MY BIG FAT ZOMBIE GOLDFISH

LIVE AND LET SWIM

MO O'HARA

ILLUSTRATED BY MAREK JAGUCKI

FEIWEL AND FRIENDS
NEW YORK

To my big brother, Matt—you're the best

A FEIWEL AND FRIENDS BOOK
An Imprint of Macmillan

MY BIG FAT ZOMBIE GOLDFISH: LIVE AND LET SWIM.
Text copyright © 2015 by Mo O'Hara.
Illustrations copyright © 2015 by Marek Jagucki. All rights reserved.
Printed in the United States of America by R. R. Donnelley & Sons Company,
Harrisonburg, Virginia. For information, address Feiwel and Friends,
175 Fifth Avenue, New York, N.Y. 10010.

Feiwel and Friends books may be purchased for business or promotional use.
For information on bulk purchases, please contact the Macmillan Corporate
and Premium Sales Department at (800) 221-7945 x5442
or by e-mail at specialmarkets@macmillan.com.

A CIP catalogue record for this book is available from the British Library

ISBN: 978-1-250-06355-7 (hardcover) / 978-1-250-06356-4 (ebook)

Feiwel and Friends logo designed by Filomena Tuosto

Originally published in the UK by Macmillan Children's Books,
a division of Macmillan Publishers Limited.

First published in the United States by Feiwel and Friends,
an imprint of Macmillan.

First U.S. Edition: 2016

10 9 8 7 6 5 4 3 2 1

mackids.com

AGENT OCTOPUS-SEA

CHAPTER 1
YOU ONLY SWIM TWICE

The giant octopus and man-sized shark danced
in time to the rap music playing over the
Aquarium loudspeakers.

"*You'll love your trip, you'll flip your lid,*
With Mr. Shark and Mr. Squid!
We're here to make your day here fun,
When you visit City A-quar-i-um!"

They finished in a kind of street-dance pose. I
was just about to clap, along with the three other
visitors that were standing there with us, when
my best friend, Pradeep, said, "That's a nice song
and everything, but it doesn't rhyme."

"Huh?" the shark replied through his bulky

rubber suit.

"'Fun' and 'aquarium' don't actually rhyme," Pradeep added helpfully.

The shark leaned menacingly toward us, so we could see our reflection in his huge white teeth.

"Not that it really matters." I gulped. "We could totally see what you were going for!" I shot Pradeep a look that said, "Shut up! Or we may end up being pummeled by dancers in sweaty fish costumes."

The guy dressed as an octopus wrapped a tentacle around Mr. Shark. "It's not worth it, dude. Let it go," he said gently.

The shark sighed. "You're right," he huffed.

They were just about to leave when Pradeep tugged on one of the octopus's tentacles.

"Excuse me?" he said. "I just wanted to clarify something. In the song you say you are Mr. Squid, but you are dressed as an octopus, so . . ." He trailed off as the giant octopus loomed over him and waved his foam tentacles.

"It's the same difference!" Mr. Squid snapped.

"Actually, the heads are a different shape and the tentacles are arranged differently and—"

"Pradeep!" I interrupted. "Shhhh!"

"That's it! I can't take this anymore!" Mr. Shark spluttered. "This is not why I went to drama school, to sing to a room full of irritating kids!"

"Dressed as a squid!" added the octopus. I think he actually flounced a tentacle as he said it.

"You mean an *octopus*," Pradeep corrected.

"I quit!" the octopus shrieked, throwing all eight arms into the air.

"Me too!" Mr. Shark added as they stormed off.

Pradeep, Sami (Pradeep's three-year-old little sister) and I watched them waddle angrily down the hall. Sami tried to copy the swish of Mr.

Shark's tail as he
stomped along.
She was wearing
a bright yellow
life jacket that she
had begged her
dad to buy her in the
gift shop. It had a big
yellow shark fin on the
back, and ever since she'd put it on, she'd been
pretending to be a shark too.

"Da-dum . . . da-dum . . . dum dum, dum
dum, dum dum . . ." Sami mumbled to herself as
she crashed into my leg and shark-bit my sleeve.
"Mwhy are msinging fishies mgrumpy?" she
added, her teeth firmly clamped together.

"I was just trying to be helpful." Pradeep
sighed.

I patted him on the back. "I don't think they
were happy here. You were just the straw that
broke the octopus's back."

"Octopuses don't have bones," Pradeep said, "so technically that would be impossible. But thanks anyway."

"Swishy fishy not grumpy," Sami said, unclamping her teeth and picking up the City Aquarium water bottle that I had used to smuggle in my pet zombie goldfish, Frankie.

It was one of those bottles that had little plastic fish and glitter suspended in a pocket of liquid, so that it looked like the fish were actually *in* your drinking water. I'd kept it ever since our school field trip here in first grade. No one would notice one more fish in there. Even an undead, brought-back-to-life-with-a-battery, green-gunk-eating zombie goldfish with hypnotic eyes.

At least I hoped not.

Pradeep shot me a look that said, "You brought Frankie to the Aquarium?"

My look answered, "I've brought him to school, to a museum, on vacation, on a camping trip, to our sports day and the school play. I'm not gonna let him miss out on a trip to somewhere fish are *actually* supposed to be!"

"Fish are supposed to be IN an aquarium, they aren't supposed to VISIT one!" Pradeep looked back.

"Not till now!" I said out loud.

CHAPTER 2

ON HER MAJESTY'S SECRET GOLDFISH

"Say hello, swishy fishy," said Sami, holding Frankie's bottle up to the piranha tank. The piranhas swam by, completely ignoring us, until Frankie smiled at them with his big jagged teeth. Suddenly, they all threw themselves at the glass in full attack mode.

Pradeep, Sami and I all leaped back and I *might* have screamed for a second.

I could swear Frankie was sniggering to himself as he swam safely in his bottle.

"Um, maybe we should move on to the next tank. I don't think Frankie is making friends here," Pradeep said.

"Good call," I replied. "Hey, how long is it until the Amazing Antonio is on?"

"Mmwant mto msee moctopus!" Sami mumbled while shark-biting my leg.

"We're meeting our dads and Mark and Sanj at the shark tank in an hour for the shark feeding, and then at the octopus tank an hour after that for the Amazing Antonio, the Octopus's Psychic Prediction Show," Pradeep answered, looking at the laminated schedule his mom had given him.

Both of our dads had been stuck on their

phones with work texts and e-mails since we'd gotten to the Aquarium. As soon as we left the shop, where they had bought Sami her shark life jacket and me and Pradeep each an Aqua Survival key ring, they'd headed to the café to work.

Sanj (Pradeep's Evil Computer Genius big brother) and Mark (my Evil Scientist big brother) had gone off together, leaving us with Sami.

It had worked out pretty well, actually, as it meant we could take Frankie out of my backpack so he could see the Aquarium properly, even if all he'd done so far was terrify a cuttlefish, spook the angelfish and provoke the piranhas.

All Pradeep and I *really* wanted to see was the Amazing Antonio anyway. For an octopus, he has a pretty impressive record for making psychic predictions. So far, he has accurately predicted the results of over twenty soccer games, five horse races, one heavyweight boxing championship, three global elections and a sudden surge in Chilean chocolate prices.

"OK, we've got time then," I said. "Let's explore."

As we continued wandering through the Amazonian section, Frankie started getting fidgety. I peered into his water bottle. His eyes were a bright zombie green and his fins were balled up, ready for a fight.

"Frankie, what is it?" I asked.

Frankie pointed to a door labeled "Staff Only" just beyond the piranha tank. It was open a crack, and there was a puddle of water on the floor. We could see what looked like tiny, wet paw prints trailing from the puddle.

"Mess!" Sami cried, shark-toddling toward the water.

Just as we were heading over to investigate, a silver-haired janitor with a square jaw and a scar across one cheek came out of the "Staff Only" door. As well as his City Aquarium janitor coat, he wore a black bowler hat and carried a tightly rolled umbrella. He looked around, then pressed a button on the side of his umbrella. It instantly lengthened and a mop head popped  out of the bottom. He quickly mopped up all the evidence, then pressed the button again and the mop disappeared back into the umbrella.

He tipped back his hat and gave us a look that said, "There's nothing to see here. Move along." Grown-up looks are usually really hard to read, but this was pretty clear.

We grabbed Sami and walked back toward the other fish tanks.

"Did you see that janitor's cool umbrella?" I asked Pradeep.

"Yes, and did you see the way he mopped up all the paw prints before we could investigate them?" Pradeep whispered back.

"Maybe he's just really tidy," I suggested.

"Or maybe he's covering something up," Pradeep added.

"Whatever it is, Frankie's eyes are *still* glowing zombie green, which means there's something fishy going on," I said. "I think we should keep an eye on that janitor."

"Agreed," Pradeep said. "There's something just not very 'janitor-y' about him."

We were walking past a huge tank of tropical fish when we spotted Sanj and Mark.

"Get back," I whispered. "Evil big brothers dead ahead."

We all ducked behind the tank.

"Do you think they could have had something to do with that puddle?" whispered Pradeep.

"Let's follow them and find out," I replied.

We crept along the side of the tropical fish tank, but when we got to the corner, Mark and Sanj were gone. All we could see was another "Staff Only" door down by the clownfish tank, along with some overexcited toddlers screaming "Nemo! I found Nemo!" and hammering on the glass. A piece of plastic tubing was propped against the wall outside the door.

"Where did they go?" Pradeep asked.

"Maybe they just wanted to avoid us?" I suggested. Then I realized it was silly to even try and think of a non-evil reason for whatever they were up to. "Or maybe they *are* planning something evil? But seriously, how evil can you be in an aquarium?"

We looked over at Sami, who was holding
Frankie in his bottle. They were both making
silly faces at the clownfish. The clownfish didn't
seem impressed.

"You're right," said Pradeep. "Let's just relax
and check out the tropical fish section."

We headed over to join Sami. Frankie was
clearly enjoying scaring the cute little clownfish
when he suddenly froze, as if he'd spotted
something suspicious.

We were just
down the hall
from a big
display
tank that
had a black
curtain
around it
and a sign
on the front
that read:

THE AMAZING ANTONIO
(THE OCTOPUS)
WILL APPEAR HERE
THIS AFTERNOON!

Pradeep and I turned to look where Frankie was looking and caught a glimpse of the silver-haired janitor slipping through another staff door, right next to Antonio's tank.

That in itself wasn't suspicious. I mean, he works at the Aquarium, right? That's what "staff" means.

But the way that the janitor looked around before he went through the door, as if he was checking to see if anyone was watching him— that *was* suspicious. That, and the way that he looked like he was talking into the handle of his umbrella.

"There's definitely something fishy about that janitor," I whispered to Pradeep.

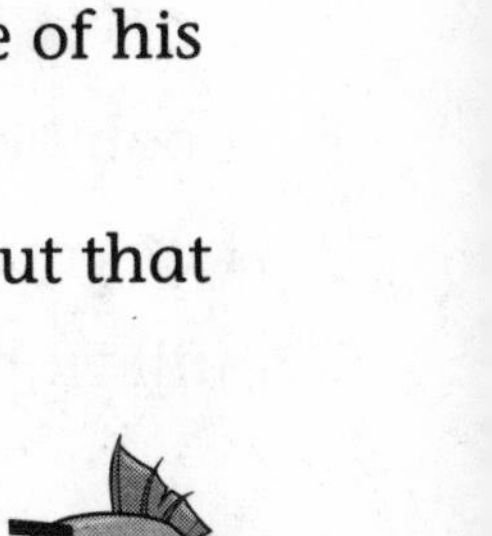

I lifted Frankie's bottle out of Sami's hands. "Is he who you're suspicious of, Frankie?"

Frankie glared at the door.

"Look, more wet paw prints!" I added, spotting a trail on the ground. The prints led into the staff area.

"OK, let's look at this logically," Pradeep said. "Shifty-looking janitor—*check*. Suspicious wet paw prints—*check*. Sanj and Mark disappearing, confirming possible presence of Mark's evil vampire kitten sidekick, Fang, who could have left wet paw prints—*check*."

"We should investigate," I said. "Frankie's zombie sense is telling us something is wrong, and he tends to be right about these things." I paused. "Not that it ever really goes well when we follow Frankie's instincts. To be honest, we usually end up being tricked by a booby trap and suspended from the ceiling . . . but you know . . . Frankie's instincts are still right."

"So are we going in?" Pradeep asked.

"Yes!" Sami said, and shark-toddled ahead of us toward the door.

CHAPTER 3

THE BOY WITH THE GOLDEN FISH

We inched open the staff door and could hear voices inside. Well, one voice, actually. It was the janitor, I guess, and he seemed to be talking to someone.

"How're you doing today?" the janitor started to say. Then, "No, no, no! Get back in the tank, Houdini. No escape tricks today."

We peered in from behind the door. The janitor was on the other side of the room behind a big tank. That's when we realized who he was talking to. Inside the tank—or rather, climbing *out* of the tank—was Amazing Antonio the Octopus.

At least I assumed he was Antonio. He looked the same as in all the online videos I'd seen of him, but I couldn't swear to it in an octopus identification lineup.

While the janitor was gently lifting Antonio's tentacles back over the edge of the tank with his umbrella, we took the opportunity to get closer.

I shot Pradeep a look that said, "Let's hide in

the closet just next to this doorway. We'll get a better view."

He nodded and we all tiptoed through the doorway and into the supply closet.

Sami, Pradeep and I peeked out again just as the janitor finished flipping Antonio's tentacles back into the tank. The octopus gave the janitor a very disappointed look.

"Did you take the lid off your tank again?" the janitor asked.

The octopus had two clear plastic boxes next to him in his tank. He used them to predict stuff. One of the boxes was labeled "YES" and the other "NO." I guess they had different labels depending on what Antonio was predicting.

He curled up in the YES box.

"You can't do that," the janitor scolded him. The octopus climbed out of the YES box.

"And look at this mess out here. I guess it's down to me to clean up all the water you spilled getting out?"

The octopus curled up in the YES box again and turned away from the janitor.

"Yeah, yeah, always down to Oddjobz to do everything," the janitor muttered. He deployed his umbrella mop again. "I'm going to need a bucket to clean all this up."

He started heading right for us but there was nowhere to go!

Light fell onto three kids' faces and one green-eyed fish as he opened the closet door.

"Argggggggggggggggghhhhh!" the janitor screamed, and dropped the umbrella mop.

"Argggggggggggggggghhhhh!" I screamed, and dropped the bottle with Frankie in it.

"Argggggggggggggggghhhhh!" Pradeep screamed, and would have dropped whatever he was carrying, but he wasn't carrying anything.

Then it started . . .

"EEEEEEEEEEEEEEEEEEEEEEEEEEEEEEE!" Sami screamed at a pitch that would cause dogs in the next county to come running.

The janitor, Pradeep and I stopped screaming and covered our ears instead. Suddenly, we had a much more pressing problem than  being caught in the "Staff Only" supply closet. How could we stop this *horrible* sound?

I tried to calm Sami down. "It's OK, Sami, you just had a scare. We're all fine!" I screamed over her screaming. But nothing worked.

The janitor looked down at us. "How long can she keep doing that for?" he yelled, still covering his ears.

"Her record is seven hours and twenty-three minutes. Then she just fell asleep mid-scream," Pradeep yelled back.

"Aha!" I punched the air. "I know what can make her stop!" I picked up Frankie's bottle and unscrewed the lid. Frankie poked his head out, fins over the side of his head, and stared straight into Sami's eyes.

The screaming stopped. We all uncovered our ears.

"Swishy little fishy," Sami said quietly, grabbing the bottle.

The janitor frowned. "Did that fish just—"

"He didn't really *do* anything," I interrupted, nudging Pradeep.

"Yeah . . . I mean no, he didn't like, *hypnotize* her or anything," Pradeep said. I nudged him harder. "Ouch, I mean . . . she just really likes our fish. Always calms her down to see him."

The janitor nodded and spoke in a low, gravelly voice. "I understand the little lady. That's why I've worked here for the last few years. It keeps me calm being surrounded by all these fish. Perfect job after such a dangerous

career . . ." He stopped himself
and a serious look came to
his face. "These areas are not
open to the public, you know,"
he scolded us. Then he smiled
and held out his hand. "I'm
Oddjobz," he said. "The name
says it all. And you are . . . ?"

Pradeep stepped forward.
"I'm Pradeep, and this is my little sister, Sami."

"And I'm Tom," I said, "and this is Frankie."
I nodded to Frankie, who was looking over
Oddjobz's shoulder at something.

"Bit of a funny thing to bring a pet fish to an
aquarium, but who am I to judge?" the janitor
muttered.

Frankie thrashed and pointed behind Oddjobz,
who turned around just in time to catch the
octopus red-handed (or red-tentacled) climbing
out of his tank again.

"My fault. I didn't put the lid back on," the

janitor said quickly, edging Antonio back into the water and pulling the heavy lid most of the way across the top of the tank.

"Why does the octopus want to get out so much?" Pradeep asked.

"I don't know . . . Maybe he misses the ocean. They caught him off the coast of South America somewhere. Then the Aquarium people spotted how smart he was and started getting him to make predictions," Oddjobz replied.

He started rooting around in a small tank nearby, from which he pulled a water-filled plastic jar containing a small, worried-looking crab. "Nearly feeding time," Oddjobz explained.

"So he doesn't like predicting World Cup–winning soccer teams or who'll be the next president of Luxembourg?" I asked. "I think that would be pretty cool."

"Sad little octi," Sami said. She walked over to the tank, still carrying Frankie in the bottle. He had clearly released her from the hypno-stare.

Sami put her hand up to the tank and Antonio put his tentacle up to meet it on the other side of the glass.

"I make you smile," Sami said. She started doing some shark-toddler impressions for him. Antonio still looked pretty sad though.

"Do you think she can communicate with the octopus like she could with the evil eel in

Eel Bay?" Pradeep's look said to me.

"No, I think she can just tell he's sad. I mean, look at him. That's one glum octopus," I answered in looks.

Sami stared into the eyes of the octopus. "Maybe octi lonely?" she said. She climbed up the stepladder to the octopus tank and popped open the lid of Frankie's bottle. "Swishy fishy play with you!" she cried, and dumped Frankie into the tank.

"Noooooooooooooooooooooooo!" we all shouted.

Well, all of us except Sami.

CHAPTER 4
THE TANK IS NOT ENOUGH

A confused-looking Frankie tumbled into the octopus tank.

Antonio took one look at Frankie and you could tell right away what he was thinking—and it wasn't "Oh, here's a fishy friend to come and play with me!" It was "LUNCH!"

Frankie's eyes glowed bright green. He poised his front fins, ready to karate-chop his way out of any attack, and bared his teeth, ready for a fight.

The octopus and fish circled each other, checking out each other's weaknesses. Suddenly, the curtain on the other side of the tank was pulled open. An announcer in an Aquarium

uniform stood in front of a surprised-looking crowd. He spoke into a microphone.

"Welcome to the octopus-feeding time at the Aquarium today. As you can see, our famous octopus, the Amazing Antonio, is about to have his lunch."

We could see through the glass on our side of the tank that the crowd was not expecting the fight of the century at feeding time.

"Now, as you probably know, octopuses are very smart, so we like to give them a bit of a challenge at feeding time so they don't get bored.

We normally give them a container that they have to figure out how to open to get their prey. Usually a lobster or a crab of some kind . . ."

The announcer trailed off as he stared into the tank at the octopus and fish locked in pre-battle circling.

"Actually, every single time I've done this we've given the octopus a jar with a crab in it . . . but apparently today we have decided to go for a special challenge and have Antonio chase and catch his prey."

We could see our dads in the crowd through the glass. They must have finished working in the cafe. Luckily they were checking their phones instead of looking at the tank.

I shot Pradeep a look that said, "Quick, duck, so they don't see us!"

As we yanked Sami off the ladder and ducked down, I was sure I spotted Mark and Sanj coming out of another door behind the crowd. They were carrying a piece of pipe or tubing with them, and

I swear I could see a little furry tail peeking out of Mark's jacket.

The announcer spoke again. "It looks like today the prey is a . . . goldfish. It's a bit of a *special* choice, but then the Amazing Antonio is a very *special* octopus."

The crowd clapped and cheered.

That's when Antonio sprang. He whipped around the tank, trying to grab Frankie. Each time Frankie tried to escape, he was slapped back down by a wave of tentacles.

Pradeep spotted a pipe in the far corner of the tank. "Frankie could get through that—look!" He pointed.

I tapped on the glass to get Frankie's attention and motioned to the exit.

Frankie looked at me, winked, then sprinted for the pipe, disappearing out of sight.

"I guess that today, the lunch got away . . ." the announcer said, and got a laugh from the crowd.

But Antonio wasn't going to give up easily. He put one tentacle into the pipe and then another and another. He was squeezing himself inside.

"He can't actually fit through that pipe, can he?" I asked Pradeep, knowing there were millions of octopus facts stored up in that brain of his.

"Well . . . an octopus that size can fit through a tube about the size of a bottle top," Pradeep replied. "So probably."

I gulped.

"Remember, octopuses don't have any bones. If their beak can fit through a hole, then they can. They are totally squishable."

"Octopus must give good huggles," Sami added.

Oddjobz had dropped the crab in the jar the moment he realized what was happening and was already up the ladder pushing the heavy lid off the tank, but the pipe was just too far away.

"There should be a filter over that pipe. Someone must have taken it out!" Oddjobz said, as Antonio disappeared after Frankie.

Pradeep and I shot a look at each other: "Mark and Sanj!"

"We have to get Antonio back," Oddjobz said, climbing back down the ladder. "If he can get through that pipe, he can get into any of the other tanks in the aquarium."

"That means he can still get Frankie!" I said. "Where does that pipe go?"

"The filtration system leads all over the

seawater section of the Aquarium. From here it will pass through the ray and skate pool, the sea star pool, the seahorse grove and then on to the . . ." Oddjobz stopped. "The shark-feeding tank."

"Well, I guess that's the end of the octopus-feeding show," came the announcer's voice. He sounded a bit confused. "See you in an hour for shark feeding, and then back here later this afternoon for the Amazing Antonio's latest predictions! *If we get him back in time, that is.*" He mumbled that last bit.

"How are we going to save Frankie?" Pradeep asked.

"Swishy fishy not playing chase with octi?" Sami said. I could see her bottom lip starting to quiver.

The last thing we needed was Sami having

a meltdown if she realized what she'd done.

I took a deep breath and said, "Don't worry, we'll get him back!" Then I looked over at Pradeep. "*Somehow,*" I added.

CHAPTER 5
FOR YOUR FINS ONLY

"Listen up, kids." Oddjobz's voice had changed into serious mode and he barked orders with precision. "We have a mission."

He pushed a button on the wall and the table top flipped over to reveal an architectural map of the Aquarium. All the pipes and tanks were marked, as well as the access points from behind the tanks.

"We all have to work together," Oddjobz said as he gathered us around the map.

"Pradeep—plot the route through the fish tanks to intercept Antonio and your goldfish."

"Yes, sir," Pradeep answered.

"You—Tom." He looked at me and I gulped.
"You're on lookout. Keep your eyes peeled for
anything suspicious while you are tracking the
absconders."

"The who?" I asked.

"The absconders . . . the escapees . . . Antonio
and the fish!" he said.

"Yes, sir," I answered.

"And you—" He turned to Sami.

She straightened up to sharky-toddler attention.

"You carry the fish's bottle so you'll be ready to put him in it when you catch him."

"Yessy, sirry!" Sami shouted, and then giggled.

"OK, I've got a route memorized," Pradeep said.

"Good," said Oddjobz. "I'll check the behind-the-scenes sections of the Aquarium to make sure they haven't come out anywhere back here, while you check the tanks that are viewable to the public. You should see them coming through the filtration pipes." He paused. "Stay focused, boys. Your fish is counting on you."

We nodded.

"And you too, shark-girl," he added as an afterthought.

We opened the staff door and ran straight into our dads, who were once again plugged into their cell phones.

"Hey, we thought we might see you here!"

Pradeep's dad said, looking up as we crashed into him. "Did you see the octopus show? We didn't spot you earlier."

"Tom, don't you think that goldfish looked a bit like—" my dad started to say, when both their phones went off at the same time.

"Sorry, got to deal with a situation at work," Pradeep's dad said, fiddling with his phone.

"Me too," my dad said, typing away.

"Did you see the seahorses, Sami?" Pradeep's dad asked, eyes glued to his phone screen.

"No," said Sami. "But sad octi and swishy fishy—"

"Let's go and see the seahorses now," Pradeep interrupted. He started walking away with his hand over Sami's mouth.

"We'll meet you for the shark feeding, OK?" I said, following Pradeep.

"Mmm," Pradeep's dad mumbled, texting away. "See you kids later."

*

"Don't you think it's strange that both our dads have had so many urgent work messages today?" Pradeep asked as we hurried along.

Sami interrupted us. "Swishy fishy!" She pointed to a flash of orange in a tropical fish tank down the hall. That kid has really good eyesight!

We ran to the tank as fast as we could, only to see a final tentacle disappear into the pipe at the far end.

"The filters on *all* the pipes between the tanks must have been removed," I said.

"But why would someone do that?" Pradeep asked. "To create a mass fish-breakout? Or just to let Antonio escape?"

"None of the other fish can fit through the pipes. Not in these tanks anyway," I said, looking at a pufferfish bouncing against the pipe entrance.

"And why isn't Antonio stopping to munch on any other fish on the way?" Pradeep added. "It's suspicious . . . in a Mark and Sanj *mostly evil* kind of way."

"But what would they have to gain from messing with the tanks in an aquarium?" I asked.

"I don't know." Pradeep sighed. "Like Oddjobz said, let's just focus on finding Frankie."

We followed Pradeep's memorized map to the skate and ray pool. It was a shallow tank of water with a plastic lid on the top so you could look at the fish from above. The water at the far end of the pool started to gurgle, and then out popped Frankie, looking over his shoulder as he swam.

"There he is!" I shouted, pushing past a startled family to press my face to the tank.

A second later Antonio spilled out of the pipe after him.

"Swishy fishy and octi having fun!" Sami clapped.

Frankie dodged the octopus's tentacles by jumping up out of the water. He leapfrogged off the back of skates and rays all along the length of the tank, while Antonio swerved in and out of the startled fish.

"It's the octopus!" the mom of the family cried.

"Is that the fish he was going to have for lunch?" asked the dad.

"He's not having this fish for lunch," I said. "Come on, Frankie!"

When Frankie got to the pipe leading out of the pool, he flipped around at the last second and grabbed the tail of a skate in his mouth. As he swam backward into the pipe, the skate became wedged into the opening, blocking it so Antonio couldn't follow.

"Good move, Frankie!" Pradeep shouted. "That should stop him."

Unfortunately for Frankie, a wedged skate was no match for Antonio's eight suckered arms. In seconds he'd pulled the skate free and had disappeared down the pipe himself.

The startled skate shook himself and swam back to his friends.

"Noooo!" I cried.

At that moment Oddjobz emerged from a "Staff Only" door and whispered, "I thought I might be able to cut them off at the cleaning hatch, but they slipped through.

Keep trying, boys . . . and shark-girl. We'll catch up with them!" He disappeared behind the door again.

"Come on, next tank!" I cried.

This section of the Aquarium was much quieter, with hardly any people milling around. We ran around a corner and Sami clapped her hands with excitement.

"Love starry-sea stars!" she squealed.

Frankie sploshed into the sea star tank from a pipe in the top corner. Sea stars were everywhere, stuck to the sides and top of the tank. Frankie didn't even pause for breath, heading straight for the exit. Just as he was about to escape, a tentacle thrust out of the pipe behind him and dragged him back.

"Frankie!" Pradeep and I yelled.

"Hello, octi!" Sami cheered.

Frankie thrashed about and managed to shake Antonio off. But by now the rest of the octopus had slipped into the sea star tank.

"What's Frankie going to do?" Pradeep said. "He's got nothing in there to defend himself with!"

Frankie looked at the starfish and then he looked at me. He winked.

"Oh yes he has," I said. "Ninja-fish throwing stars!"

Frankie gripped a sea star in his teeth and flung it at Antonio. It sailed through the water with precision, clocking Antonio right in the eye.

The octopus flapped his tentacles and squinted at Frankie. If I could read octopus looks, I'd swear Antonio said, "Bring it on, small fighting fish!"

Frankie let off a volley of flying sea stars that spun through the water like a scene from a fishy kung fu movie. Each one rocketed toward its target. This time, though, Antonio was prepared. All eight tentacles shot out and grabbed a spinning sea star. Then Antonio hurled them right back at Frankie!

Frankie legged it (or whatever fish do that's fast but doesn't involve legs) and shot through the exit just as sea stars started sucker-splatting behind him.

"Phew!" I sighed. "Antonio can't follow Frankie now. He's blocked the pipe with sea stars!"

"Um . . ." Pradeep tapped me on the shoulder and pointed to Antonio peeling off the stunned sea star from the pipe entrance. "I don't think Antonio heard you."

Antonio disappeared through the opening in an instant.

"Naughty octi and fishy!" said Sami crossly,

pushing her face against the glass tank.
"Poor starry-sea stars. Must be all dizzy."

"Never mind the sea stars," cried Pradeep,
tugging Sami's arm. "We've got to find
Frankie!"

CHAPTER 6
LICENSE TO SWIM

We ran down a ramp and passed some tanks containing crabs and creepy glow-in-the-dark fish. Where could Frankie have gone? What if Antonio got him in one of the pipes?

The next tank on Pradeep's mental map was the seahorse enclosure, but we couldn't see Frankie or Antonio anywhere.

"See seahorsies!" Sami cried.

Then Pradeep spotted a separate tank. "Seahorse Grove," he read from a sign on the wall as Sami shark-swam over to peer inside. "This is a Baby Seahorse Nursery. Please Be Quiet. No Shouting. No Photography. Do Not

Wake the Babies!" There was a picture of a sleeping baby seahorse underneath.

Suddenly, Frankie plunged into the seahorse grove, with Antonio right behind him! The two were just about to fight when Sami tapped gently on the glass and pointed to the sign with the picture of the sleeping baby seahorse. They paused and looked around at the tiny figures of seahorses snoozing peacefully all around them.

Sami put a finger to her lips.

Gently Frankie and Antonio tiptoed around the sleeping baby seahorses, until they got to the pipe on the far side.

Then Frankie shot through the entrance of the pipe with the octopus right behind.

"Not again!" Pradeep cried.

We raced along, following the pipe to the next section of the Aquarium. Suddenly, the pipe disappeared into the wall, taking Frankie and Antonio behind the scenes. Just next to the pipe was another staff door. But as we looked closer, we saw that someone had taped a note just below the "Staff Only" sign, so it now read:

STAFF ONLY

NO MORONS EVER! GOT IT?

I shot Pradeep a look: "It has to be Mark who wrote this!"

Pradeep's look said back, "But why would Mark be in the 'Staff Only' section of the Aquarium?"

My look responded: "I don't know, but I'm sure it's something evil."

Then Sami tugged on my shirt. "Why you doing the funny secret-look thing?" she said in looks. "There's only me here."

"OK," I said out loud. "We've got to find out what Mark is up to *and* find Frankie. Agreed?"

"Agreed," Pradeep said. "I bet Sanj is in on this too."

Sami nodded.

We cracked open the "Staff Only" door and listened. Voices were coming from a room inside, farther down a corridor.

"The 'sending the dads fake work problems to keep them busy' plan seems to have worked perfectly!" we heard Sanj say.

"Yeah, and the little morons won't mess things up for us either," we heard Mark reply.

"They'll never find us in here! I even put up a special 'No Morons' sign so they'll definitely stay away."

"You put up a *what*?" Sanj replied.

Water swooshed through the pipe over our heads in the direction of Sanj and Mark's voices. We followed the sound, tiptoeing along the corridor.

"Our guests are about to arrive," Sanj's voice said. "I have two blips on my Fish Pipe Tracking app."

The door to Mark and Sanj's hideout was open, so we hid to one side and peeked in.

Mark was sitting on a large leather chair, wearing his white Evil Scientist coat with Fang, his evil vampire kitten, sitting proudly on his lap. Sanj was sitting on a normal chair at a table nearby, entering something into his computer tablet.

Sanj looked up at Mark. "What are you doing *now*?"

"I wanted to have the right look for when we capture them. What do you think?"

Even I have to admit, he did look pretty evil.

"Welcome, Mr. Octopus," Mark went on. "We've been expecting you!" He stroked Fang and did his trademark evil laugh.

"It's OK." Sanj shrugged. "It would probably have been more effective with a white cat."

Fang hissed.

"Don't you listen to him, my evil little kitty-witty," Mark cooed.

Sanj sighed and shook his head. "Can we *please* just get on with the plan? Step One—we

capture the octopus . . . and as luck would have it, the zombie goldfish too."

"Step Two—feed the moron fish to Fang," Mark interrupted.

"No, no, no!" Sanj shook his head. "We discussed this when we devised our back-up plan just in case those pesky brothers of ours manage to find out what we're up to. No feeding the fish to Fang. We might need him *alive*."

Mark and Fang both sulked.

"Step Two is where we coerce the octopus into believing that we will emancipate him and thus get him to use his innate psychic abilities to divulge those winning digits!"

Sanj clapped his hands in a particularly evil way.

"Hunh?" said Mark.

Sanj sighed. "We trick the octopus into thinking we'll free him so he gives us the information we want, even though we're not actually going to free him at all!"

"Oh, right, yeah," Mark said, and slipped Fang into his lab-coat pocket. Then he jumped up and moved a cart holding a large, water-filled fish tank so it was just underneath a pipe hanging from the ceiling.

Sanj stood up and held an open jar under the spout of the pipe. "Any . . . second . . . now!" he said.

At that instant, Frankie swooshed out of the pipe and landed right in Sanj's waiting jar.

"Swishy fishy! Noooooo!" Sami shouted, and ran into the room.

Sanj clamped shut the lid of the jar and held it out of Sami's reach.

"Let Frankie go!" I yelled, racing in just as Antonio tumbled out of the pipe after Frankie and landed in the tank.

Mark slammed shut the lid and locked it.

"Well," Sanj said to Mark. "I guess your 'No Morons' sign didn't work. But no matter. We'll just have to resort to the backup plan."

Mark rubbed his hands together. "I *love* the

backup plan. That's the one with the sharks, right?"

"Sharks?" I echoed as Pradeep raced into the room and skidded to a halt next to me.

Pradeep pointed down. "Um, Tom. Does this floor mat we're standing on look weird to you? Because we have a really bad habit of getting stuck in booby traps and—"

Whooosh!

The next thing we knew, Pradeep and I had been scooped up by a giant net and were hanging from the ceiling!

CHAPTER 7
EVIL KITTENS ARE FOREVER

"Don't you dare say 'I told you so,' Pradeep," I mumbled, as I dislodged his sneaker from next to my face. "Why does this always happen to us?"

"We should probably just check for booby traps when we walk into any room," Pradeep said. "You know, trap doors, circles of rope, statues with mechanical arms . . .”

“Good plan.” I nodded.

“Are you done?” Sanj shouted up to us. “Can we get back to the evil plan now?” He had Sami under one arm and was carrying the jar with Frankie in it in the other. Sami was wriggling and kicking to get free.

“Naughty Sanj!” she yelled. “Put me down!”

“Hold still,” Sanj said. He handed the jar with a thrashing Frankie inside to Mark, and wrapped a bungee cord around Sami and the chair to keep her in one place.

“That ought to hold you until we can deal with the octopus,” he muttered.

Mark put the jar down on Sami’s lap. She stared at Frankie through the glass. His eyes were a bright, hypnotic green, but nothing was happening.

Sanj tapped the glass of the jar. “Hypno-proof. No ‘swishy fishy’ chanting for me today.”

Then Fang jumped up onto Sami’s lap. She

stared at Frankie and licked her lips.

"Can't I feed the fish to Fang instead of the sharks?" Mark whined. "She looks really hungry."

"We *agreed* on the sharks. Every time we try to feed the fish to Fang it goes wrong. Besides, sharks just have more impact," Sanj replied. "And they're cooler than kittens."

Fang growled at him.

"So why do you want Frankie *and* the octopus?" I yelled, playing for time while we tried to figure out a way to escape.

"Your moron fish was just a bonus," Mark said with a sneer. "It's the octopus we're after. We set up the whole thing—taking out all the filters on the pipes to lead the octopus directly to our evil hideout. It took us ages, *and* we had to keep sneaking past that creepy janitor guy."

"It seems a kinda long-winded way to trap the octopus," Pradeep said. "Antonio's always climbing out of his tank on his own. You could have just walked in and taken him."

"We know that Antonio is prone to escaping," snapped Sanj. "What do you think we are? Fools? *That's* why we came up with the plan. If we had just walked in and stolen him, the Aquarium would have got the police involved. But if the octopus escaped through, say, some faulty filters in the tank systems, no one could possibly blame us. They'd probably just fire that old janitor for not doing his job properly."

"No! Oddjobz loves his job," I whispered to Pradeep.

Sanj carried on. "You see, I've been observing Antonio on the Aquarium CCTV cameras that I hacked into. That octopus can understand and communicate far more then they know. I've seen him read signs, watch guards entering codes on keypads and then punch in the same codes when he's trying to escape . . . I've even seen him disable security cameras."

Frankie was still thrashing in his jar on Sami's

lap as Fang circled, just in case the jar fell on the floor.

"But when I saw him predicting soccer scores and election results, I realized this was not only a very intelligent octopus. It actually has *psychic* powers. We had to be certain, so Mark and I snuck into the Aquarium last weekend and ran tests using playing cards. The octopus had a near flawless rate of predicting the card I was holding. This octopus's talents are wasted on picking the winning team in some infantile soccer match."

"Though I still wanna know if the Barrington Bounders will win today," Mark added.

Antonio made a thumbs-down sign with two of his tentacles.

"Oh, man . . ." Mark mumbled.

"I've reconfigured Sami's 'Say It, Spell It' to be a waterproof communication device for the octopus," Sanj said, holding up the toy. "Whatever the octopus types will be vocalized through this wireless speaker." He clipped a pink plastic box to the side of the tank.

"Naughty Sanj broke my toy!" Sami shrieked.
"Bad Sanj!"

"It's all in the name of science, Sami," Sanj
said. "Now let's see if Antonio can work out how
to communicate
with us." He
lifted the lid
and dropped
the device into
the tank with
the octopus.
Immediately
Antonio started
typing away on the keypad.

The pink speaker burst into life with a weird
robotic voice. "My name is Juan Antonio Ignatius
Carlos Octopus, but you can call me Antonio. I
was captured off the coast of South America last
year. *Gracias* for your communication device.
It is *mucho* helpful. Excuse my grasp of English.

I am translating from Octopus to Spanish to English. It can get jumbled. I long to get back to *mi casa*, my home . . . the sea."

Pradeep pushed a bit of net away from his eyes and stared down at his evil older brother. "Wow, for once you've done something not 'mostly evil,' Sanj!"

Sanj looked offended. "What do you mean?"

"Your discovery of this communication method with the octopus. It's a major scientific breakthrough! You could benefit animals all over the world. Now we can show this to the Aquarium people and they'll release Antonio back into the wild."

Sanj threw his head back and gave an evil wheezy laugh, and Mark joined him.

"Mew, mew, mew, mew, mew!" echoed Fang.

"Are you kidding?" Mark said.

"There's money to be made from this octopus," Sanj snapped. "The only person I want to benefit from Antonio's psychic powers is me!"

"And me," Mark added.

"Yes, yes," Sanj mumbled. "And him. I just had to make sure Antonio could communicate complicated thoughts with me. I don't care what he's feeling or if he wants to go home. Boo-hoo! Poor little octopus!" He tapped the glass of the tank. "You might be extraordinarily smart and frustrated by the staggering array of ordinariness around you, which I completely understand as I constantly feel that way myself, but I *honestly . . . don't . . . care.* All I want *you* to do is make me money."

The octopus started typing things very fast on the keypad. Sanj quickly pressed mute on the speaker.

Pradeep stared down at the keyboard from our position hanging in the net. "It looks like he's saying something in Spanish, but they're not

words we've learned in school," he whispered.

"Ignore that!" I whispered back. "We need to think of an escape plan, and fast!"

CHAPTER 8
QUANTUM OF FISH FOOD

"I would like to remind you there is a small child present," Sanj snapped at the octopus, and pointed at Sami. "I'm going to turn the speaker back on now, and I do not care to hear any of those words again."

Antonio looked over at Sami. "Sorry," came the robotic voice.

Sami smiled back at him.

"Now," Sanj carried on. "You have a single job to do for us, Mr. Octopus. You are going to predict the winning lottery numbers for tonight's Billion Dollar Rollover win. With that money Mark and I can build the evil lair we've always dreamed of."

"Yeah, with sharks and everything," Mark added. "And a kitten palace with more string then you could ever shred, Fang. And loads of fish to eat . . . even if they're not zombie goldfish."

Fang sharpened a claw on the ground and grinned.

"Why would the octopus agree to that?" I asked.

"Will you release him back into the ocean?" Pradeep said.

"Of course not!" Sanj answered. "Why would I throw a money-making octopus back out to sea?"

"Then I don't think the octopus is going to want to help you," I said.

"That's where *you* come in." Sanj smiled.

He pressed a button on the wall and the net Pradeep and I were trapped in started to travel along a track on the ceiling.

"This is how they transport really heavy fish

from one tank to another," Mark said.

"I've programmed it to head for the shark tank," Sanj added. "Shall we see if it works?"

Frankie thrashed like mad in his jar and Antonio pushed at the lid of his tank, but there was no way out.

Sanj and Mark followed us, Mark pushing Antonio's tank on the cart and Sanj pushing Sami, still tied up in her chair with Frankie and Fang on her lap.

I could see us getting closer and closer to the shark tank. It was HUGE. The glass on one side faced into the "Staff Only" section of the Aquarium. The other side had a black curtain hanging in front of it, just like the one that was in front of the octopus tank earlier. This must be the shark-feeding tank. Only today, *we* were on the menu!

I stared into the tank. The glass on the back wall looked like a mirror from up here.

I shot Pradeep a look that said, "I think the

back of the tank is one-way glass, like they use in cop shows."

"It looks like it," his look replied. "I guess that's so the audience can't see what's behind the tank."

The net slid along until it came to a stop over the exact center of the shark tank. Shark fins sliced through the surface of the water, and we could see the distinctive outline of hammerhead sharks.

"Hammerheads!" Pradeep said with a gulp. "They're known man-eaters."

"I don't really want to be shark lunch," I whimpered.

"Or dinner or a snack!" Pradeep added. "Hang on. I have a plan . . ."

He whispered something and we both started searching through our pockets.

"OK, Mr. Octopus, this is how it works." Sanj spoke over us. "Give us the winning lottery numbers for tonight's big draw . . . or we lower the morons into the tank."

"¿Qué? Morons? ¿Idiotas?" came the robot voice from Antonio's tank.

"I should have added a translation algorithm," muttered Sanj. "I'll lower the *boys* into the shark tank." He rolled his eyes. "For a psychic octopus, you are being very obtuse."

No sound came from Antonio's tank.

"Right, that's it!" said Sanj. "Lower the morons!"

"For real?" Mark cried. Then he started to

whisper, but we could still hear bits of what he was saying to Sanj. It sounded like, "Blah, blah, blah, just wanted to scare the octopus, blah, blah, blah, not *really* gonna dunk them, blah blah, blah, real sharks and all?"

"Just go along with it!" shouted Sanj.

Mark pressed another button on the wall by the tank and the net started heading for the water.

"I can predict that the boys are actually in *pequeño* danger," the robot voice suddenly said. "The sharks are well-fed and used to having divers in their tank. I predict the boys will remain calm and use the sharp whittling edge of their Aqua Survival key rings to cut themselves free as soon as they hit the water. They will then simply swim to the escape ladder located by the rear south corner of the tank, and get away. I will not help you."

"Gah!" shouted Sanj. "Mark, stop the net."

Mark pressed another button and we ground to a halt.

Sanj squinted up at us as we quickly tried to

hide our Aqua Survival key rings.

"Wow, how did Antonio know that?" I said from the swinging net. "I mean, not that it was EXACTLY our plan or anything"—I looked at Pradeep, who was still shoving his key ring back in his pocket—"but it was kinda close."

Sanj turned back to Antonio. "OK, let's try something different."

He grabbed the jar with Frankie in it from Sami's lap, then climbed up the emergency ladder to the tank and started unscrewing the lid.

"We know how much you wanted to munch on this delicious zombie goldfish. So either you

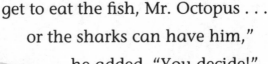 get to eat the fish, Mr. Octopus . . .

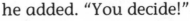 or the sharks can have him,"

he added. "You decide!"

CHAPTER 9
SKY-FIN

At that moment, Fang leaped off Sami's lap, bolted up the ladder and knocked the jar from Sanj's hands.

"Stupid cat!" yelled Sanj as Frankie and the jar both tumbled into the shark-infested water. He leaned back to get away from Fang's razor-sharp claws and toppled off the ladder with a thud.

Fang looked like she was going to jump in after Frankie, but as soon as the tip of one of her paws touched the water she pulled it back with a frightened "Mew!" and jumped onto the net Pradeep and I were trapped in.

"Frankie!" I shouted from the net, while trying to avoid Fang's claws digging into the top of my head. "Zombify them!"

The sharks started to circle around Frankie. His eyes glowed green and he curled up his fins, ready for a fight.

"I don't think he can hypnotize them!" Pradeep said. "He can't look into both eyes of a hammerhead at the same time!"

"Nooo! Swishy fishy!" Sami shouted over us. She was wriggling so much that she had gotten herself completely tangled up in the elastic bungee cord that Sanj had used to secure her to the chair.

"Mark, tie her up again properly!" Sanj shouted from the floor where he'd landed.

Antonio thrashed angrily in his tank. He grabbed the "Say It, Spell It" and started typing, but before he could get any words out Sami leaped up off the chair.

Sami was an expert wriggler. Somehow she had managed to slip out of the cord at the exact moment that Mark went to retie it. She ran between his legs, circled around and then dashed underneath the chair, causing Mark to become tangled. Stretched to its elastic limit, the bungee cord suddenly pinged back, pinning Mark's arms to his sides and trapping him in the chair.

"Hey, not fair. Let me outta this!" Mark shouted.

Sanj had just pulled himself to a sitting position and was rubbing his head when Sami stepped on him to get to the first rung of the ladder.

"Ummmph!" he spluttered as she clambered over him.

"Sami!" yelled Pradeep. "Stop!"

But she didn't stop. In fact, Sami pretty much forgot to stop altogether when she reached the top of the ladder.

"Fishy!" she shouted as she tumbled toward the water.

"Sami!" yelled Mark, Sanj and Pradeep.

"Got you!" I cried, as I reached through the

net and *just* managed to grab the tip of her shark-fin life vest.

Now we were stuck in a net dangling over a shark tank, with Sami dangling below us.

CHAPTER 10
TOMORROW NEVER DIVES

The black curtain on the public side of the tank was still closed as Sami hung facedown above the tank.

"Help!" she whimpered.

"I've got you, Sami," I cried. "I won't let you fall."

Below us, Frankie was swimming for his life, dodging sharks as they swiped past him.

The octopus typed furiously on the keypad. There were words: "Little shark-*niña*! I must help the child who was kind to me." Then there was a long sequence of numbers.

"Yes!" Sanj shouted, leaping up and running

toward Antonio's tank. "The lottery numbers."

He lifted the lid to free Antonio the octopus. "Now you can eat the fish!" he said.

Fang hissed.

Sanj immediately picked up his tablet and started typing.

"Aren't you gonna free me first?" Mark pleaded from his chair. "I can get Sami down while you do the computer stuff."

"Yes, yes, in a minute!" Sanj muttered. "I need to concentrate when hacking."

Meanwhile, Antonio squelched out of his tank, across the floor, and climbed the side of the shark tank with his suckers. He heaved himself over the top and in seconds he was in the water beside Frankie, surrounded by sharks.

"Please don't eat my zombie goldfish!" I yelled down to him.

Frankie narrowed his eyes at Antonio, ready to take on the octopus *and* the sharks.

"Help!" Sami whimpered again.

Antonio looked
at Frankie. Then
he pointed up
at Sami with
one arm, at
himself with
another, and
did some kind
of complicated sign
language, waving his other six legs.

I could see Frankie relax. He nodded.

"I think Antonio has proposed a truce,"
Pradeep said, "so together they can rescue Sami.
Or at least that's what I think he said. I've never
seen octopus sign language before. He might
have said he likes surfing and sushi. I guess we'll
find out?"

Frankie started swimming faster and faster in
tight circles, creating a whirlpool of water as he
zipped past the hammerheads' noses. While the
sharks were distracted, Antonio climbed back up

the inside of the tank. When he got to the top, he threw out two of his long, stretchy tentacles and managed to grab Sami's dangling hands.

"Octi sticky!" Sami squealed, as Antonio used his suckers to start pulling her, and the net we were in, to the side of the tank. As soon as Sami was at the edge, she scrambled down the ladder.

Meanwhile Pradeep and I used our Aqua Survival key rings to saw harder than we ever had in our lives. Finally, the net gave way and we clambered down. Fang leaped after us, hissing at Antonio and heading straight for Mark.

Above us, Antonio was trying to dip his

tentacles into the water to grab Frankie, but every time he did, a hungry shark snapped at him. The octopus stopped and rubbed his head thoughtfully with two of his tentacles. Then he plopped into the tank.

"Frankie!" Pradeep and I whispered.

"Octi!" Sami mumbled.

Sanj was ignoring us, typing away, while Fang appeared to be trying to chew Mark loose from his bungee cord.

Suddenly the black curtain opened on the other side of the tank and we heard the announcer's voice saying, "Welcome to feeding time at City Aquarium's special shark-feeding tank! This is where the sharks have their meals while we clean out their bigger tank at the front of the Aquarium. Let's see what the sharks are having today!"

Frankie was looking wobbly now, probably from swimming so fast, round and round in circles. The sharks were getting closer with every swipe. Meanwhile, Antonio had wrapped himself around the head of one of the sharks, holding its mouth closed with his stretchy arms, and was hanging on for dear life.

"Wait a minute!" the announcer said. "Is that the same fish as before? And the Amazing Antonio! That can't be right . . ."

Frankie pulled out of his whirlpool and swam up to Antonio's shark. Then he circled its head as fast as he could, using his zombie stare the whole time.

"I think he's figured out a way to hypnotize the hammerheads!" Pradeep shouted. "Look!"

As soon as the first shark was hypnotized, Antonio grabbed another, and Frankie started circling again.

Moments later, all the sharks were gently moving through the water, staring at some seaweed with one eye and up the nostril of the nearest shark with the other.

"It worked!" I said.

Antonio shook fins with Frankie, picked up the empty jam jar and climbed out of the tank onto our side of the one-way glass.

The announcer stared at the mesmerized sharks and the lone goldfish now swimming around the tank. "Does that fish look like it's gloating to you?" he mumbled. "And what happened to Antonio? Maybe the sharks aren't that hungry today. Let's look in on them later." He quickly shut the curtain again.

Just when I thought things were under control,

Fang finally bit though the bungee cord. It snapped back with a *twang*, freeing Mark but sending Fang flying across the room toward Sanj, who was huddled over his computer, furiously typing away.

"Miaoooowwww," Fang screeched as she slammed into the back of Sanj's chair and dug her claws into the closest thing at hand to steady herself: Sanj.

"Owww! Get your menacing kitten off me!" Sanj shouted. "We are so close to completing our plan!"

As Mark stomped over to Sanj, Frankie swam to the top of the tank and Antonio used the jar to scoop him up out of the water.

"Right," Mark grumped, picking up Fang and stroking her. "I'm free and Sami's safe, but the morons have escaped and the stupid octopus and fish HAVEN'T been eaten by the sharks! This backup plan sucks! You better have the money or—"

"I needed to concentrate!" Sanj snapped.
"It took a while to bypass the Lottery website
security as we are underage, but now that
I've hacked into the system and created a new
account we are ready to go. Let's enter those
winning numbers!"

"Stop!" I yelled. "We can't let you!"

Sanj turned around and stared at us in
surprise. "You could have told me they'd
escaped," he muttered, glaring at Mark.

"I just did." Mark glared back.

"I stopped listening to you after 'I'm free.' You
really must warn me when you have anything
important to say," Sanj huffed. "Just stop them!"

"Pradeep, let's try and grab the computer," I
said in looks. "Sami, you distract Mark."

They both nodded.

"Now!" I shouted. Pradeep and I ran toward
Sanj, but Mark blocked us easily, grabbing each
of us under one arm. Then Sami tried to crawl
through his legs, but Mark clamped his knees

closed, trapping her. He was a one-man wall of defense!

Fang sat on Mark's head and swiped at us as we dodged her claws.

"Finally, you're doing *something* right," Sanj said to Mark with a smirk. "I'm just entering the final details. When they announce the rollover winner tonight . . . it will be us!"

"Shark lair, here we come," Mark added.

"Frankie!" I called with the squished breath from my Mark-squeezed lungs. "Help!"

CHAPTER 11
A VIEW TO A TANK

Frankie shot a look at Antonio. The octopus
nodded, wound up his arm like a pitcher and
threw the jar with Frankie in it over Mark's head
and right at Sanj.

The plastic jar knocked Sanj on the head and
water splashed all over the tablet. It fizzed and
sparked. Sanj dropped it to the ground and the
screen went blank.

"No!" Sanj screeched, while Frankie clung
onto Sanj's bangs and fish-slapped at his nose.
"You've broken the connection. I'll have to log in
and enter the lottery numbers all over again."

Meanwhile Antonio had slithered over to

Mark, squelched up his legs and was shoving his tentacles into Mark's nose to try and get him to drop us.

"GET THE MORON FISH OFF ME!" Sanj shouted.

"EEEEWWWW!" Mark screamed. He dropped us to the floor, grabbed the bungee cord and wrapped it around Antonio's tentacles before shoving him into his tank and slamming the lid closed. Then he turned to Sanj and Frankie. "You are definitely cat food this time, fish!"

"Mew!" Fang agreed, jumping on top of Antonio's tank for a better view.

At that moment, Sanj picked up the tablet from the floor and used it to thwack Frankie like a ping-pong ball toward Mark.

Frankie crashed to the ground and lay stunned on the floor.

Pradeep, Sami and I all leaped forward to try and grab him, but Mark was faster. He picked up the dazed goldfish and flung him toward Fang, who stood on top of the tank with her mouth wide open.

"Noooooooooooo!" Pradeep and I yelled.

"Swishy fisheeeeeeee!" Sami shouted.

Suddenly, a spinning bowler hat come hurtling through the air toward Frankie. In one swoop, it scooped up Frankie and boomeranged

back to

its owner,

Oddjobz,

who was

leaning

against the

"Staff Only"

door.

"That is NOT the way we treat fish in *this* aquarium," Oddjobz boomed. He glared at Mark and Sanj. "Bring me that jar, shark-girl," he added in a softer voice.

Sami scurried over to Sanj, grabbed the jar

and brought it to Oddjobz, who gently put Frankie inside. "I think he needs a drink, don't you?" he said to Pradeep and me.

We ran to get some water.

"Now I think *you two* have a lot of explaining to do." Oddjobz pointed his tightly rolled umbrella at Sanj and Mark.

Fang leaped off Antonio's tank and into Mark's pocket, meowing a panicked meow.

Sanj and Mark shot each other a look that said, "Let's get out of here!"

A second later, they were running for a fire exit on the far side of the room. But before they could even reach the door handle, Oddjobz pressed a different button on his umbrella and it shot out two lengths of rope with weights on each end. The ropes tangled around Sanj and Mark's ankles, sending them crashing to the floor.

"Oh, man!" yelled Mark. "Now I'm tied up again. This REALLY sucks!"

Oddjobz sauntered over to them. "As I was saying, you two have some explaining to do," he said as he hung his umbrella over his arm and readjusted his hat.

"Who wants to start?"

By now Pradeep and I had filled Frankie's jar with water and untied Antonio, who was poking at Frankie with a tentacle. But Frankie wasn't poking him back. In fact, Frankie wasn't moving at all!

"Swishy fishy sick," Sami said.

"Not to worry," Oddjobz replied. "I've seen this in fish before, when they've had a shock. You need to move the water around the jar to get it flowing through his gills."

I started to swish the water around in the jar.

"It's best if it's shaken, not stirred," Oddjobz added.

I gently shook the jar instead, and Frankie started to come around.

"What did you say you did before you worked

at the Aquarium?"
Pradeep asked.

"That's classified."
Oddjobz smiled.
He looked down at
Frankie, who was now
swimming around.

"Works every time," he said.

Antonio picked up the "Say It, Spell It" toy
keyboard from inside his tank and started to
type. "I predict that the fighting fish will recover
well, but he will have *mucho grande* headache,"
the robotic voice announced.

Frankie nodded.

"Poor swishy fishy," Sami said, snuggling the
jar. "I look after you."

Frankie rolled his eyes at us but let Sami kiss
his head when he thought we weren't looking.

"Thanks, Mr. Oddjobz, for saving Frankie," I
said.

"And thanks, Antonio, for saving Sami and

for saving us,"
Pradeep added.
"And for not
eating Frankie."

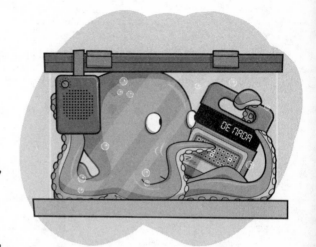

Antonio typed,
"*De nada*, no
worries," and
waved his tentacles.

"Antonio"—Oddjobz leaned down to talk to
the octopus—"I'm really sorry, but you have an
appearance to make out there in the Aquarium."

Antonio shrugged his tentacles since he didn't
really have shoulders to shrug with.

"Octi sad," Sami mumbled.

"You're coming too," Oddjobz said to Mark
and Sanj. He helped them to stand up, then
tied them together with the bungee cord before
releasing their ankles. "I wish there was a way to
avoid it, Antonio," he said, looking back over his
shoulder as he worked, "but there's a big crowd
gathered. Word has spread around that you got

into the shark tank and put on quite a show.
You're more popular than ever."

"Hang on, that's it!" Pradeep suddenly shouted.
"You're more popular than ever. *That's* why it
might work!"

CHAPTER 12
GOLD-FIN-GER

Pradeep whispered his plan to us all.

"What do you think?" he asked.

Antonio typed, "It's worth a try."

"Listen, while you're working all this out you might as well let us go, right?" Sanj said, squirming in the bungee cord.

"Yeah, you can't keep us like this," Mark added. "It's cruelty to Evil Scientists."

"And Evil Computer Geniuses," Sanj added.

"I'm used to taking the law into my own hands," Oddjobz

said, straightening his hat. "I'll deal with the consequences."

He radioed the security team through a hidden speaker in the umbrella.

"That is the coolest umbrella ever," Pradeep said, staring at the buttons on the handle. "Do they sell these in the gift shop?"

"Standard issue from my old job." Oddjobz smiled. "You're pretty good at coming up with plans though, kid. Maybe you'll get one for yourself one day . . . when you're older." He winked.

Oddjobz escorted Mark and Sanj while Pradeep held Frankie and I pushed Antonio in his tank on the cart. Sami carried a very unhappy Fang (whom we'd removed from Mark's pocket after we'd caught her trying to bite through the bungee cord).

We opened the door to the public bit of the Aquarium and headed toward the octopus display area. When we got there we saw that a

huge crowd had gathered in front of the tank, and the announcer was standing in front of the curtain. "There's just going to be a short delay . . ." he was saying. "I'm assured that one of our staff is bringing Antonio back safely as we speak . . ."

"That's right." Oddjobz's voice boomed out across the room. Everyone turned around to look. "Here he is." Then he nodded to Pradeep and me and whispered, "You're up."

Pradeep cleared his throat. "Thank you, ladies and gentlemen," he said in a loud, clear voice that Mrs. Loubinhall, our school drama teacher, would have been proud of. "We have an announcement to make."

Just then we spotted our dads in the crowd. At the exact same moment, they spotted us . . . including Mark and Sanj tied up in the bungee cord.

They pushed to the front of the crowd. "Where were you at the shark feeding?" my dad said. "We were worried!"

"And what are you doing with our sons? Let them loose immediately," Pradeep's dad said to Oddjobz.

"I'm sorry, sirs, but your sons have been involved in an incident," he said.

Both dads' faces dropped into a look that clearly said, "Oh no, here we go again."

Oddjobz explained that they had trespassed in restricted areas, contaminated exhibition tanks, and endangered the well-being of customers and the Aquarium fish. A security guard came over and Oddjobz handed the boys over to him. "I'm afraid they'll have to work off the money to pay for everything that they've damaged," Oddjobz continued.

"This is all just a misunderstanding," Sanj protested.

"It was the stupid moron fish's fault!" Mark muttered.

"Oh, and a kitten was illegally brought onto the premises. There'll be a fine for that too,"

Oddjobz added. The
security guard put
on protective
gloves before
Sami handed
him a hissing
Fang.

Sami
shark-swam
up to her dad and
pretended to attack his legs. Then Antonio the
octopus reached out of his tank and patted her
on the head.

The crowd gasped.

"Me make octi friend, Daddy," said Sami.

"What?" said Pradeep's dad.

Pradeep stepped forward and handed the
"Say It, Spell It" to Antonio in the tank. "The
Amazing Antonio has something to say to you
all," he announced.

The computer voice started speaking as

Antonio typed. "My name is Juan Antonio Ignatius Carlos Octopus, but you can call me Antonio. I was captured off the coast of South America last year. *Gracias* for your communication device. It is *mucho* helpful. Excuse my grasp of English. I am translating from Octopus to Spanish and then to English. It can get jumbled. I long to get back to *mi casa*, my home . . . the sea."

The crowd gasped again and the Aquarium announcer leaned back against the wall and wiped his forehead with his sleeve. He was as white as a sheet.

As soon as Antonio stopped speaking, that was my cue. I started clapping and shouting "Bravo!" Then Sami, Pradeep and Oddjobz joined in. The dads started clapping too, even though I'm sure they didn't know what they were clapping for. Soon the whole audience was clapping and cheering.

Pradeep stepped forward again. "Thank you

for participating in City Aquarium's totally interactive 'Talking Octopus Experience.' This show was designed to entertain you, including octopus and stunt goldfish chases throughout the day, a pretend shark fight and now the 'Amazing Antonio the Talking Octopus Experience'!"

The cheers from the crowd got louder.

"I knew it was staged," one lady said.

"Yeah, that goldfish must have been one of those plastic motorized fish," a man replied.

"I bet it was all CGI," a boy added.

Frankie wriggled angrily and tried to jump out of his container, but I clenched my hand over the lid.

"The show was to entertain," Pradeep said. "But the message that we want to teach you is much more serious. City Aquarium is committed to sea-animal welfare and believes that *some* sea creatures need to be in their natural habitat to be happy. So as part of that commitment they are going to release Antonio back into the South American ocean!"

The crowd cheered even louder and clapped. The Aquarium staff were patted on the back and congratulated.

Pradeep's dad went up and shook hands with someone in a suit who must have been the Aquarium manager. She looked shocked as Mr. Kumar said, "What a fantastic way to get everyone involved in your commitment to help sea creatures return to the wild!"

The announcer pushed through the crowd and stood next to the manager. "The crowd loves this idea. It's great for our image!" he whispered.

The manager stepped forward and smiled at Pradeep. "Yes, of course, City Aquarium is always looking for creative ways to teach and entertain." She looked at Oddjobz and Antonio. "Some more creative than we ever thought possible." She faced the crowd again. "So City Aquarium *will* release Antonio back into the ocean."

The crowd went wild.

The announcer stepped forward this time.
"Now if you would all like to follow me back to
the shark-feeding tank, I'm assured that they are
just about to feed, for real, this time. And there's
not a goldfish or an octopus in sight." He headed
off, followed by most of the crowd.

"Mr. Oddjobz," the manager started. "I don't
know how you did this, but the Aquarium has

not had such good publicity for years. Things have gone wild on social media and we've had people visiting the website and booking visits all afternoon. Even the TV news want to do a story!"

"It was really the idea of these two boys here," Oddjobz said. "Oh, and shark-girl." He winked at Sami, who shark-thrashed the fin on the back of her yellow life jacket.

"Well done, boys . . . and shark-girl," the manager said kindly. "Wherever did you get a stunt goldfish like this one?" She pointed at Frankie in his jar. "We'd love to have him here as an exhibit in the Aquarium."

"I don't think he'd like it much," I jumped in. "He's happy where he's living now."

Frankie thrashed in his jar and pointed to a tank on the wall. "Although he might accept a small fish tank as a thank-you present."

Frankie thrashed again.

"I mean, a medium-sized tank," I added.

"Of course." She smiled.

Then the manager motioned to our dads. "Unfortunately, we also need to discuss how your older sons will work off the money for the damage that Mr. Oddjobz tells us they caused."

"Excuse me," I interrupted. "But I think I have an idea!"

CHAPTER 13

DIVE ANOTHER DAY

Mark and Sanj stomped out of the entrance of the Aquarium in their Mr. Squid and Mr. Shark outfits.

"I can't believe I have to spend every Saturday singing for annoying children dressed as a giant octopus who has been inappropriately named Mr. Squid!" Sanj moped.

"I think I changed my mind about wanting an evil lair with sharks. If I ever see another shark, it will be too soon!" Mark huffed.

Fang hissed as Mark pulled her out of his shark hood, dressed as a mini piranha.

"I think the piranha look really suits Fang,

actually,"
Pradeep said
to me.

We were
waiting at
the exit to the
Aquarium
for the dads
to come out
with Sami.

She was skipping and shark-swimming at
the same time. Not an easy thing to achieve,
really.

Sami skipped/shark-swam over to us while the
dads spoke to the security guards about Mark
and Sanj's working hours. "This was best trip
ever!" She beamed.

A moment later Oddjobz appeared at the exit
with Antonio in his tank.

"Wow, you're going right away?" Pradeep
asked.

"I don't think Antonio wants to wait any longer. Besides, today's my last day working here too. I just quit." Oddjobz explained, "I love this job, but I think it's time I had a change of scene. I told the Aquarium that I would make sure that Antonio got back to the ocean safe and sound. So we're heading off now for a flight to South America so I can take him out into the ocean where he belongs. Then maybe I'll retire and go sailing."

"I'm glad we got to meet you," I said, shaking his hand.

"Are you sure you can't tell us what you did before?" asked Pradeep.

"If I told you, I'd have to wipe your brain so you didn't remember anyway." Oddjobz smiled. "But I'm very good at keeping secrets, so your zombie goldfish secret is safe with me."

"How did you know . . . ?" Pradeep started to say.

"It's classified," Oddjobz said, and tipped his

hat. "Come on, Antonio, we've got a plane to catch."

"*Adios*," Antonio typed on the "Say It, Spell It."

Sami ran up to Antonio and reached out her arms. He gave her a big squishy hug good-bye over the side of the tank. "*Adios*, sharky-*niña*," he typed with two of his spare arms.

Finally, Frankie flipped up out of the jar I was carrying and high-fived one of Antonio's tentacles.

"*Adios*, fishy *amigo*," Antonio typed. Then he turned off the speaker, typed out a sequence of numbers and handed the "Say It, Spell It" to Oddjobz.

"Well, I guess this is good-bye," said Oddjobz. "You kids take care."

We waved as he started to push Antonio's tank away.

"Are you done with speaking now?" we could hear Oddjobz asking the octopus. "I guess you won't need this in the ocean." He was just about

to dump the "Say It, Spell It" in a bin when he
looked at the screen.

"Maybe we should stop and get a lottery
ticket on the way to the airport?" we heard him
mutter. "I'm feeling lucky."

MY PET'S GOT TALENT

CHAPTER 1
A WILD RIDE

"WHEEEEEEEEEEEEEEEEEEEEEEEEEE!"

Sami, my best friend Pradeep's little sister, raced down the hill on her scooter toward the school gates. "Hang on, Toby!" she shouted to the terrified tortoise that was wedged into a small yellow bucket hooked over her handlebars.

"Bumpity-bump-bump coming up!"

"Sami!" I shouted from my bike, pedaling hard to keep up. "Slow down!"

"We'll get there in time, don't worry!" Pradeep panted, speeding along behind me.

Sami's scooter hit the bump and took off. "Yaaaaaay . . . Flying bit!" she squealed. But Toby the tortoise had not followed instructions and hung on (not that tortoises have a natural ability to hang on to things). Sami's scooter bumped back to the ground with a *thunk*. She looked up to see Toby spinning through the air above her head.

"Toby flying?" she said as she stared at him in disbelief. My bike hit the bump and I took off too. I stretched out my arm to try and grab the terrified tortoise but I just managed to knock him with my elbow instead.

"Pradeep!" I yelled as I crashed back down. "Tortoise! Incoming!"

Pradeep was on it, but as he too hit the bump, he lost his grip on his handlebars and was thrown up into the air. Somehow he managed to grab Toby with one hand and pull himself back onto his bike with the other. Even Pradeep would have calculated that the likelihood of all that working was a zillion to one.

I slammed on my brakes and spun around to see Pradeep land hard on his bike seat.

"ARRRRRGGGGGGGGGGGHHHH!" he screamed, while his look said, "My bottom feels like it's been hit by a train, a bus and a 747 all at once!" When he had finally stopped screaming, he got off his bike and cowboy-walked over to Sami.

"Next time we say 'Slow down,' can you please slow down?" he scolded, holding out Toby, who had very sensibly disappeared inside his shell.

"Sorry, Pradeep," Sami said, taking the tortoise. "Sorry, Toby," she whispered into his shell.

Toby popped his head out, and if I could read tortoise looks I'd swear Toby was saying, "Can I just go back to my grass now, PLEASE?"

"I wish Cousin Joe was around to take Toby and Sami to this audition," Pradeep muttered as

he walked back to his bike. "Toby's *his* tortoise. The TV show's called *My Pet's Got Talent*—not *My Cousin's Pet's Got Talent*." He rubbed his backside and winced.

Across the road in the school parking lot were two huge trailers with satellite dishes on the top. The writing on the sides read:

TTP
TRANS-ATLANTIC TELEVISION PRODUCTIONS

A line of people stretched from the door of one trailer all the way to the school gates.

"We should probably get in line if we want to get into the auditions," Pradeep said, still rubbing his bottom.

"Yaaaaay!" Sami squealed again. "Toby TV star!" She wedged the tortoise back in the bucket and grabbed Pradeep's hand to cross the road.

"*My Pet's Got Talent*," I mumbled. "Hey, this is one of Solomon Caldwell's TV shows! Do you

think he'll remember us from the school play he came to?"

"I think Solomon Caldwell meets about a million people a year," Pradeep answered.

"I guess." I sighed.

"But I bet no one else hypnotized him with a zombie fish, trapped him in a baker's hat and nearly hit him with an arrow with a goldfish hanging off it," Pradeep added.

"That's true!" I said. "Hey, speaking of fish . . ." I smiled and took off my bike helmet. Hidden inside was Frankie, my pet zombie goldfish, in a plastic bag of water.

"You brought Frankie to the auditions?" Pradeep sighed. "You're not going to get him to zombify people, are you?"

"Of course not," I said.

"But . . . does he have any other talents?" Pradeep asked. "No offense, Frankie," he added quickly.

"I don't know," I said, slipping Frankie inside

my jacket as I started to cross the road. "But I'm sure he'll come up with something. Besides, I couldn't leave him at home."

There was no way that I was risking leaving Frankie in the house with my Evil Scientist big brother, Mark, and his equally evil but cute little vampire kitten, Fang. Although, come to think of it, I hadn't actually seen either of them at all this morning.

"But whenever you bring Frankie *anywhere*, there's always trouble!" said Pradeep.

"Don't worry," I said with a grin. "Frankie will be on his best behavior. Won't you, Frankie?"

Frankie shrugged.

"Why don't I think this will end well?"
Pradeep muttered.

CHAPTER 2
IN LINE FOR STARDOM

We parked our bikes and Sami's scooter in the bike shed and joined the back of the line. Ahead of us were kids with all kinds of talented pets. There was a boy with a beagle called Charlie that could roller-skate. Another kid had a beret-wearing ferret called Tugger that was painting with its tail. There was even a girl with a rabbit that was pulling another rabbit out of a top hat. She told us they were called Siegfried and Roy.

Sami held Toby tight in her hands. "Toby got talent," she said.

"I don't really think that crawling fast can be

called a 'talent,'" Pradeep said.

"Toby is telepopping tortoise," Sami replied.

"She's got a point," I agreed. "It is kinda like he teleports. I've never seen a tortoise that can make it down a driveway and across two gardens in the time it takes to get my bike out of the shed."

"Will you guys never learn!" a familiar voice said from behind us. "They are always listening out for things that can't be explained. Never admit, never deny!"

"It couldn't be?" both Pradeep and I said at the same time.

We turned around and there was Geeky Girl. Her mom runs the convenience store down the road and she has a thing about conspiracy theories, but she was totally cool about helping us save Frankie from our evil big brothers one time.

"Hey, Glenda," Pradeep said. Geeky Girl rolled her hand up into a fist.

"I mean, 'Hey, Geeky Girl,'" he corrected himself. "How've you been?"

"Good, thanks, Brainiac." She let her mouth curl up into a slight smile and punched Pradeep on the arm. "Hey, little dude," she added, winking at Sami.

"Have you still got your budgie?" I asked, just as a green and yellow bird flew down from the rooftops and perched on her shoulder like a tiny pirate's parrot.

"Yup, Boris is cool too," she said.

"Are you entering Boris into *My Pet's Got Talent* for his ability to fly and hover just over your shoulder?" asked Pradeep.

"His levitating skills," I corrected.

"Ssshhhh! They are always listening," Geeky Girl said, looking around for the "they," I guess.

"If you're not entering him for his levitating skills, what else does he do?" I whispered.

"I'm here to investigate. There's been some strange stuff going on. Pets not being able to perform their talents at the auditions," Geeky Girl replied. "Something fishy's going on and I want to check it out."

Frankie started thrashing around inside my jacket, probably because he heard Geeky Girl say "something fishy."

Geeky Girl frowned at me. "OK, so either you have one serious case of indigestion or you've got your fish in there?"

She leaned over, unzipped the top of my jacket

and looked in. "Hey, Frankie, how you doing?" she said with a smile. Frankie rolled the bag up and fish-high-fived her through the plastic.

"Can we get back to the 'something fishy' going on?" I said.

"Sounds like the pets just got stage fright," Pradeep said. "Why is that suspicious?"

"Everything out of the ordinary is suspicious," Geeky Girl replied. "You've just got to watch out for the signs."

"There isn't a 'sign' for everything—" Pradeep started.

"So what other talent does Boris have?" I interrupted.

"Show them, Boris." Geeky Girl nodded at the budgie and he cleared his throat.

"Ahemmm. *Caaaw, caaaw,* caw-caw-caw-*caaw*-caaw, caw-caw-caw-*caaw*-caaw, caw-caw-caw-caw!"

"It's the theme to *Star Wars*!" Pradeep and I said together. We *have* to stop doing that.

"Birdie sings good," Sami added.

"Thank you," said Geeky Girl.

"But birdie not talented like Toby." Sami patted the tortoise on the head and set him down by her feet.

"Look!" said Geeky Girl, punching Pradeep on the shoulder. "A sign!"

"Ow!" he rubbed his arm. "A sign that someone's watching us? A sign of an evil plot we didn't see? What kind of 'sign' now?"

"I think she means *that* sign," I said, pointing to an actual sign just ahead of us at the side of the line.

PET SCREENING AREA

All pets must be screened for contaageous dissneezes before going into audition area

MANDITORRY

"Oh, *that* sign," Pradeep mumbled, turning red. People were taking their pets into the school building on the left and then rejoining the line farther down when they came out.

"I don't remember the website mentioning anything about screening pets for diseases," I said.

"And I don't think that's a very official sign. 'Contagious,' 'diseases' and 'mandatory' are all spelled wrong!" Pradeep added.

"We should check it out," Geeky Girl said. "I could send Boris on a recon mission."

Just as I was about to say "Hunh?" Pradeep came in with "Good plan: he can check out the area from above."

My confused "Hunh?" turned into a knowing "Ahhhh." Then it turned into a "Whaaaaa?" when something lifted up my left foot.

I looked down and saw Sami crawling along the floor, looking under our feet, other people's feet, the rabbits' top hat and pretty much everything else she could find.

"What's wrong, Sami?" Pradeep asked.

"Toby telepopped bye-bye," she snuffled. "He's gone."

"Sami!" said Pradeep. "I thought you were keeping an eye on him!"

Geeky Girl and Pradeep started looking around for Toby while I unzipped my jacket so Frankie could help.

He immediately thrashed and pointed in his plastic bag like a tiny, orange, scaly pointer dog.

That's when we spotted the little kitten with huge eyes and stupidly sharp claws and teeth disappearing through the door of the school building leading to the "Pet Screening Area." And she looked like she was pushing something oval and green with her nose.

"Fang?" Geeky Girl, Pradeep and I all said together.

"Toby!" Sami yelled.

CHAPTER 3
TORTOISE-NAPPED!

Frankie immediately threw himself onto the floor and started rolling his bag of water after the evil vampire kitten.

"Wait, Frankie!" I scooped him up by the top of the bag.

"We can't rush in without a plan," Pradeep explained. Frankie stopped thrashing, but his eyes still glowed bright green.

"Naughty evil kitty," Sami said.

"I have a plan!" I said. "We get a helicopter to fly over the building, drop us on to the roof and then we rappel down the walls, swing in through the window and take Fang by surprise!"

Geeky Girl and Pradeep looked at each other.

"Or we could tunnel under the building," I went on, "and plant some exploding bubble gum under the floor. When the gum explodes, Fang and Toby will get caught in the sticky bubble-gum mess and all we'll have to do is unstick Toby and get out of there!"

Geeky Girl rolled her eyes. "Could we come

up with a plan that is not the plot of an action movie or a cartoon?" she said.

"Can you get exploding bubble gum in real life?" Pradeep asked.

"I don't know but—" I started to say, when I was interrupted by Geeky Girl's glare. (If you don't think a glare can interrupt you, you haven't met Geeky Girl.)

"We are not using exploding bubble gum," she growled. "But the flying-over-the-building idea is actually OK. Boris could fly up to the window of the school to see what he can find out. He could take Frankie with him, in case there's any trouble. If anyone sees them, they'll just think goldfish-lifting is Boris's special talent."

"Will fishy and birdie be OK?" Sami asked.

"Boris and Frankie will look out for each other—won't you?" Geeky Girl said. Boris bobbed his head and Frankie winked. "We'll head in from down here," she carried on.

"OK, let's do it!" I said.

The girl with the rabbits had just come back out of the scanning exit. Pradeep and I took Sami over to play with the bunnies until we got back.

"There's nothing weird in there though," Rabbit Girl said to us. "Just a scanning machine. My bunnies got the all-clear so we're ready to audition." She smiled and handed a carrot to Sami. "Do you want to help me comb out the bunnies' fur with conditioner so that they're all pretty?" Sami nodded and tried to smile.

"I think our tortoise wandered in there," I said. "Can you hold our place in the line? We'll be back in a minute."

"Find Toby," snuffled Sami through a mouthful of carrot.

Geeky Girl, Pradeep and I ran to the doorway while Boris picked up the top of the plastic bag with Frankie in it and headed for the window.

There was no sign of Fang but there was something odd. There was lettuce all over the floor.

"Toby loves lettuce," Pradeep said.

"Fang must have lured Toby in here with the lettuce leaves and then pounced!" Geeky Girl added.

"The leaves look nibbled until you get to the steps," Pradeep said, inspecting a leaf like he was Sherlock Holmes in *The Case of the Missing Tortoise*. "But Fang couldn't carry Toby up the steps on her own. She obviously had help."

"Mark!" we all said together.

"My Evil Scientist big brother strikes again." I sighed.

"This 'saying words at the same time' thing is starting to get seriously annoying," Geeky Girl mumbled.

"Sorry," Pradeep and I said together.

Then I said, "Anyway, that means Mark is upstairs with Toby."

"And Frankie and Boris," Pradeep added. "Come on!"

We all ran up the stairs at full speed. It was only when we reached the top that we heard the creepy laugh echo through the stairwell.

"Mwhhaaa, haa, haa, haa, haa! Well done, Fang. Who's an evil kitteny-witteny? So tortoise, go on . . . do your thing!"

There was a noise like something sparking and buzzing.

We tiptoed to the open doorway and peered through. It was one of the science classrooms. The lab tables were pushed back against the walls and two box-shaped machines stood in the center of the room. Both machines had strong lids made of metal with some kind of keypad attached and clear sides. Boris and Frankie were nowhere to be seen, but Toby was inside one of the boxes and Fang was in the other, purring and sharpening her teeth. Wires ran from Toby's machine to a junction box and then to the machine that Fang was in.

"Well then?" said Mark's voice.

Toby just sat there chewing a lettuce leaf.

"That's it?" Mark huffed. "That's your talent? You *eat lettuce*? Man, standards are low for this year's show."

"We've got to get Toby out of there," I whispered to the others. "I don't trust Mark."

"There's no way he's scanning the pets for contagious diseases," Geeky Girl muttered.

"At least whatever he's doing doesn't seem to hurt the pets," Pradeep said.

While Mark's back was turned we snuck into the room and hid behind a big cabinet. As soon as the buzzing stopped, Mark walked over to Toby, opened the lid using a secret code and took the last bit of lettuce out of his mouth.

Then Mark walked over to Fang and opened her box. He handed her the lettuce and she chomped it down in one bite.

"Did that kitten just eat lettuce?" Geeky Girl whispered.

"Yup," I replied.

"You know what this means . . . ?" Pradeep said. "That scanning machine just transferred Toby's lettuce-eating talent to Fang!"

CHAPTER 4

ATTACK OF THE FLYING BUDGIE

"Mark must have done the same thing with all the other pets too!" Geeky Girl whispered.

"But why?" I asked.

Suddenly, we heard, "*Caaaw, caaaw,* caw-caw-caw-*caaw*-caaw . . ."

"*Star Wars?*" Pradeep and I said in looks.

Boris swooped down over our heads toward the machine containing Toby. He was still carrying Frankie in his bag of water.

Mark dashed over and blocked their way.

"You're too late!" he cried. "Or maybe . . . you're right on time!" He swung around and picked up Toby like he was a baseball. "Hey,

fish, catch!"—and he
hurled Toby at Boris
and Frankie. Boris
swerved, but the
edge of Toby's shell
just caught him. He
flapped and let go
of Frankie's bag.

"Frankie!" I screamed.

"Boris!" Geeky Girl
screamed.

"Toby!" Pradeep screamed.

"Morons?" Mark screamed.

I guess he was a bit surprised to see us.

Pradeep flung himself across the room toward
the back wall just as Toby landed in a basket of
sponges.

Geeky Girl lunged for Boris as he flopped
down inside Toby's now empty box, but Mark
got to him first and slammed down the lid.

I was heading for Frankie. His bag had

splatted as it hit the ground and he was flapping around in the puddle of spilled water. While I was looking for something to put him in, Fang pounced! In a flash she had picked up Frankie by the tail and was over at the box with Boris inside. Before Geeky Girl even realized what was happening, Mark flipped open the lid and Fang dropped Frankie inside.

"Hypnotize him, Frankie!" I shouted as Mark banged down the lid.

Frankie's eyes glowed green as he thrashed around, unable to get free.

"No chance." Mark smirked. He tapped the glass. "Hypno-proof. My own little addition to this model of scanner." He laughed a really scary evil laugh.

Geeky Girl pulled on the lid. "It's locked! What's the code? Let them out!" she shouted.

By now Pradeep had rescued Toby, and together we raced toward the box.

"That's it!" Geeky Girl rolled up her sleeves

and slammed her fist into her palm. "No one messes with Boris." Just as she was about to knock Mark's block off, or at least give him a good punch in the arm to think about, Fang jumped toward us with lightning speed. She had some kind of cable in her mouth.

"Look out!" I cried. But it was too late. Fang ran around us until Pradeep, Geeky Girl and I were completely tangled up in the cable. Then she leaped across the room and into the other scanner.

"We know what you're up to and you can't get away with it!" Pradeep yelled.

"Mwhaaa, haa, haa, haa, haa!" Mark laughed. "I think I just did. Ready, kitty?" he asked Fang.

"Mew, mew, mew, mew, mew, mew," said Fang. If I didn't know better, I could have sworn that was an evil kitten laugh.

Mark threw a switch on the junction box between the scanners.

"Please! Frankie needs water. Let them out!" I shouted over the buzzing, crackling noise.

"Let them go!" Geeky Girl yelled. "You were nice last time we met! I even made you tea!"

The buzzing seemed to hit a peak, and then faded out.

Fang smoothed down her static-charged fur while Mark walked over to the scanner with Boris and Frankie inside and unlocked the lid. Boris flew out, clutching Frankie in his claws.

"He needs water, Boris, find some!" I shouted to the budgie.

"Go, Boris," Geeky Girl said as we pulled at

the cable around us. Boris took one look back and then headed for the window.

"Meeeeeew?" said Fang.

"It's OK, kitty," said Mark, walking over to Fang's scanner and letting her jump onto his shoulder. "We don't need them anymore. There's nothing they can do to stop us now. I'll make sure you get to eat the fish . . . and the bird later!"

"That's especially evil. Even for you!" yelled Pradeep, still pulling at the cable.

"Thank you," said Mark. "You know, I totally didn't plan to get the budgie, let alone the stupid fish, into my Mega-Evil Talent-Transfer scanner." He flicked his white Evil Scientist coat out behind him. "I've already transferred plenty of pet talents to Fang. Definitely enough to get her on tonight's *My Pet's Got Talent* live TV show and win. Then, when I get to meet all the national finalists and scan their pets too, there will be no stopping me. I'll win the prize money fair and square. Well, fair and square for *me*." He couldn't resist throwing in an evil laugh at that point.

"I'll finally have enough money to build a proper evil lair, order anything I want from *Evil Scientist* magazine, and go to Wicked Wally's Evil Adventure World next summer. But now *you* guys have made this soooo easy. Fang is going to sail through today's auditions . . . but I'm going to save her most special talent of all until the live TV show tonight. Then we can use it on everyone that tunes in to watch the show—can't we, evil kitty-witty?" he cooed. "As well as winning

the prize money in the grand finals, I'll have an audience of evil minions to do my bidding. Result! Mwhaaa, haa, haa, haa, haa!"

It was then that we noticed that Fang wasn't sitting on Mark's shoulder anymore; she was levitating just above it.

And her eyes were a hypnotic zombie green!

CHAPTER 5

AN EVIL PLAN A DAY KEEPS THE BLUES AWAY

"You took their powers as well as their talents!"
I gasped. "Quick, everyone, close your eyes so
Fang can't hypnotize you!"

We all screwed our eyes up tight.

"You won't get away with this!" Geeky Girl
said.

"Hey, you morons interrupted me and now I
forgot what I was saying," snapped Mark.

"You were explaining your evil plan in a long-
winded way that will probably help us to come
up with an idea of how we can try and stop
you," Pradeep answered.

"Oh, yeah, thanks!" said Mark. "Anyway, Sanj

and I made these scanners out of some old CAT scan machines that the hospital was throwing away. It was the name 'CAT scan' that gave me the idea. I could scan stuff into my cat!" He flicked up the collar of his white coat and smiled. "You can tell me how much of an Evil Scientist genius I am now."

"You're an evil genius who can't spell 'contagious,' 'diseases' or 'mandatory,'" muttered Pradeep.

"Sanj usually does the spelling stuff," Mark huffed. He punched his fist into his palm.

"I knew my Evil Computer Genius big brother would be involved somehow," Pradeep sighed.

"Shame he actually ended up catching something contagious from the building where we swiped the scanner," said Mark. "But they say he'll only be in quarantine for another two weeks. I told him I'd take a selfie with Solomon Caldwell when we win and send it to him."

"So that's why Sanj has been video-calling

wearing a hazmat suit from boarding school! He said it was because he was in a play and that was his costume!" Pradeep said.

Mark looked at his watch. "I've got to get this kitten to her audition." He smiled. "You guys just hang out for as long as you want. I'll put a 'Scanning Room Closed' sign out front so you don't get disturbed." Mark picked up the "Closed" sign from a table and walked through the door, with Fang still hovering slightly above his left shoulder. We heard the lock click shut and then footsteps going down the stairs.

"I really hope Boris found some water for Frankie!" I said. "He didn't look good!"

"I'm sure Boris will have saved him. He's a very smart bird," said Geeky Girl. "Now let's concentrate on getting out of here. We are locked in and tied up. Any ideas on how to get out of this?"

"We could shuffle over to the window, attach one end of the cable to the curtain pole and then push ourselves out. The cable would slowly unroll as we fell so that we would only have to drop the last couple of feet to the ground," Pradeep said.

"Good plan," I said. "Except for the throwing-ourselves-out-of-the-window bit."

"Or we could . . ." Geeky Girl began, "just wait here for Boris to fly in through the window carrying Frankie in the little yellow bucket from Sami's scooter, which is cunningly filled with water and rabbit fur conditioner. Boris would then dump the bucket on top of us and we

could use the slippery conditioner to slide out of the cables."

"Like that's gonna happen . . ." I started to say, when I noticed that Geeky Girl was looking at Boris flying toward us across the room, holding Sami's small yellow bucket in his claws. Frankie was peeking out of the top and waving.

"Whaaa—" I began, just as Boris dropped the bucket. The water splashed all over us, making us slippery enough to wriggle free of the cables.

"OK, I get that you

saw Boris coming with the bucket," Pradeep said as he attempted to pick up an equally slippery Frankie. "But how did you know that there was conditioner in the water?"

"I have an extremely developed sense of smell." Geeky Girl shrugged. There was a slightly awkward silence.

"Let's get Frankie back in some fresh water and get out of here," I said, changing the subject. "Are you feeling OK now, Frankie?" I asked as I filled up the bucket from a sink on one of the lab tables. "I mean, after the whole scanning thing?"

Frankie squelched out of Pradeep's hands and into the bucket with a splash, then shrugged and nodded.

"We need to get downstairs and stop Fang from getting into the auditions," Pradeep said as he dried Toby's shell with some paper towels.

"Before it's too late," Geeky Girl added as she shook the door handle. "It's no good. Mark definitely locked it from the outside."

Pradeep had already tucked Toby into his jacket and picked up the roll of cable that had been wrapped around us. He carried it over to the window. "No one will see us if we go out this way," he said.

"Pradeep, I thought we vetoed the throwing-ourselves-out-of-the-window plan as, you know, I would like to get through the day with most of my bones in one piece?" I said.

"Don't worry. This is Plan B." Pradeep nodded. He handed one end of the cable to Boris, who clutched it in his claws. "OK, Boris, fly over there and hook your end onto the metal loop on that fence post," he said.

Boris flapped away carrying the cable and managed to hook it on the post. Pradeep pulled until the cable was taut. Then he tied it to the curtain pole using one of the really complicated knots he knows from camping all the time.

"Now all we have to do is slide down," he said.

I looked at the distance from the window to

the parking lot below. "All the way down there?" I gulped.

"Cool plan, Brainiac," Geeky Girl said. "I'll go first." She grabbed the cable. "It's really slippery from the conditioner!"

"Exactly," Pradeep replied. "That means less friction for sliding down the wire."

"Yeah, but it also means we can't get a grip on it properly," she said.

"That's what these are for," Pradeep said, and pulled out three wooden coat hangers from behind his back. "They were in the cabinet by the door." Pradeep smiled.

Geeky Girl grabbed a hanger and hung it on the slippery cable. "See you on the other side!"

she shouted as she pushed off.

"Wait!" Pradeep shouted. "I forgot to say, let go before you hit the post!"

CHAPTER 6
THE GREAT ESCAPE

"Awesome ride!" shouted Geeky Girl, letting go just before the hanger crashed into the fence post. "Come on down!"

"OK, Pradeep," I said. "Why don't you go next with Toby, then I'll send Frankie in the bucket. I'll come down last."

Pradeep grabbed a coat hanger, hooked it onto the cable and climbed onto the windowsill. "Here I go!" he yelled, but stayed sitting on the window ledge, not moving an inch.

"You've gotta actually push off, Pradeep," I whispered.

"I know." Pradeep's voice quivered a bit. "It all

looked fine from inside. From out here, I'm not as convinced about this plan."

"Geeky Girl was fine," I said. "Come on. One . . ." I counted.

"Two," Pradeep and I said together.

"Three," I said on my own, and Pradeep stayed perched on the windowsill.

Pradeep gripped the hanger tightly. "I just can't."

"Sure you can," I said. "Let's count again and you'll go on three."

"One," I said as Frankie leaned out of his bucket and nipped Pradeep on the butt.

"Ooooowwwwccccccchhhhh!" Pradeep yelled as he slid down the cable, letting go safely at the bottom.

"You're not very patient, are you, Frankie?" I shook my head. I unclipped the handle of his bucket, hooked it over the cable and slid Frankie down to Pradeep.

"Come on, Tom!" Pradeep yelled as he unclipped Frankie's bucket.

I grabbed my hanger and pushed off. "Geronimoooooooo!" I shouted as I shot down the cable. I remember seeing the post coming up very fast and thinking, "There's something I was supposed to do right about now . . . ?"

Below me I heard Pradeep and Geeky Girl shouting, "Let go! Tom, LET GO!"

With a second to spare I remembered that

"letting go" was exactly what I was supposed to do. I dropped to the ground and the hanger clattered into the fence post ahead.

"Now we've got to get to Mark!" I said, standing up.

We all took off. I carried the sloshing bucket with Frankie inside, and Boris clung onto Geeky Girl's shoulder as she ran.

We got to the audition trailer just as the girl with the rabbits was coming out. Sami was with her, wearing the rabbits' top hat. Pradeep took Toby out of his jacket and handed him to Sami.

"Toby back!" Sami cried, snuggling him close.

"Sorry it took us so long," I panted to Rabbit Girl.

"Yeah, we got kinda tied up!" Geeky Girl added.

"It doesn't matter," said Rabbit Girl with a sniffle. "We totally blew the audition anyway. It's like my bunnies didn't remember any of their act! They couldn't do one magic trick."

The kid with the roller-skating beagle was sitting outside the trailer too, putting Band-Aids on his dog's legs. "Yeah," he added. "It's like my dog couldn't balance at all anymore."

"Tell me about it!" said a voice from behind us. The boy who owned Tugger, the beret-wearing painting ferret, pulled out a canvas with a stick figure drawn on it. "I tried telling the judges he's going through a minimalist period, but they just said it wasn't very good." The boy scratched his disappointed-looking ferret behind the ears. "Earlier he was painting French Impressionist sunsets!"

Pradeep, Geeky Girl and I all exchanged a look that said, "The scanner!"

"I'm really sorry to hear about that," Pradeep said. "But we've got to go in for our audition now."

"You'd better hurry," Rabbit Girl said. "They looked like they were starting to close up."

"Thanks again for watching Sami," Pradeep

said as he took Sami's hand.

Frankie splashed me from his bucket. He did not want to wait another second to catch Fang and Mark. "Let's go!" I cried.

We raced around to the entrance of the audition trailer, just as the person inside was hanging up a sign that read:

CHAPTER 7
A STAR IS SCANNED

"The auditions can't be closed!" Geeky Girl protested with her hands on her hips. Boris flapped his wings and cawed.

"We've come with our pets to try out for the show," I said, holding up Frankie in his bucket.

"Toby is telepopping!" Sami added, holding out her tortoise.

"I'm sure your tortoise is very good at whatever *telepopping* is and your pets are very sweet," the woman said as she crossed off several items on a clipboard and adjusted the walkie-talkie on her belt. "But after an entire day of pets with absolutely no talent *at all*, we have managed to find the most talented pet I've ever seen!"

"You wouldn't by any chance be talking about a kitten, would you?" Pradeep asked.

"Not just *any* kitten. This kitten managed to paint a beautiful French Impressionist sunset while roller-skating, doing magic tricks, eating lettuce . . ." She paused. "I admit, we might ask her to cut the lettuce bit in the televised performance." She continued her list. "She even blew bubbles in the shape of the Mona Lisa and meowed the theme tune to *Star Wars*!"

Frankie thrashed hard in his bucket and Boris the budgie flapped angrily on Geeky Girl's shoulder.

"And you know the weirdest thing?" the woman added. "When I looked back at the video it looks like the kitten's actually doing it all while levitating an inch off the ground!" She shook her head. "It must be an illusion. But it will look *amazing* on TV."

"So where is this kitten and her owner now?" I asked.

"We want to congratulate them," Geeky Girl said, rolling up her fingers into a fist.

"They've gone through to the make-up trailer to get ready for tonight's show," the woman said. "Solomon Caldwell is going to be *so* happy!"

Frankie gritted his teeth and squinted at the woman. Then he jumped up out of his bucket and landed with a wet *thwap* on her face, glaring into her eyes. He was trying to hypnotize her! But his eyes didn't glow green and the lady didn't start staring up anyone's left nostril with one eye or looking at the wall with the other. She didn't even mumble "swishy fishy" once!

All she did was yell, "AAAAAARGGGGHHHH! Get this fish off me!"

I scooped up Frankie and dropped him back into his bucket just as two big security guards appeared.

"These kids are banned from the recording of the show!" she shouted as she wiped her face on her sleeve. "I want them out of here, pronto!"

One of the security guards pointed at the gates. The other just stood there and looked scary.

"Thank you for having us," said Pradeep in his best talking-to-a-teacher voice. "We were just going anyway." He grabbed Sami's hand and we all walked as fast as we could to the gates with the security guards right behind us.

"OK, let's get the kitten through make-up and into the school hall for the recording tonight," crackled a voice from one of the guard's walkie-talkies. "I want everything ready for when Solomon Caldwell arrives!"

Frankie stared at me sadly as the guards slammed the gates behind us. He kept squinting his eyes like he was trying to force them into his green zombie stare.

"It was the scanner, Frankie! I'm sorry," I whispered.

"It scanned your powers into Fang," Pradeep added.

Frankie stopped squinting and stared at us with wide eyes.

"Don't worry. We'll get your powers back," I said. "Somehow!"

"Caw!" added Boris.

"But we only have a couple of hours before filming starts," Pradeep said.

"And even if we *can* get back in there, Frankie can't zombify the TV crew into stopping the show," Geeky Girl added.

Frankie sank to the bottom of his bucket

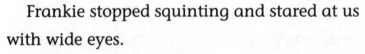

and heaved an underwater sigh.

"Don't be sad, swishy fishy," said Sami, patting him on the head.

"Basically, we need to get Frankie's powers back from Fang *before* we can stop Mark's evil plan. If we don't, Fang will zombify the whole country when the show is broadcast tonight!" I said.

Just then I saw Pradeep's face get that "I'm figuring out something really, really complicated in my head and there's no room for anything else so I'm switching off all unnecessary functions" look. In other words, Pradeep went blank like there was a power cut to his face. He stayed like that for a full minute—and then suddenly the power switched back on.

"We can't get Frankie's powers back from Fang *before* the show is broadcast," he said. "But we can get Frankie's powers back *during* the show instead."

CHAPTER 8
TALENT TRANSMISSION 101

"I don't get it," Geeky Girl said. "And I get most things, so it's kinda bugging me. How can you get Frankie's powers back *during* the show?"

"We'll need to get one of Mark's scanners on to the stage," said Pradeep. "We then need to create some kind of 'talent-transmission' device, or satellite dish, that we can use to transmit the talents back to the affected pets in a kind of scatter-gun broadcast. All we have to do is get Fang into the scanner and all the pets that have lost their talents into the transmission radius of our device."

I stared blankly at Pradeep.

Geeky Girl frowned.

Sami hugged Toby. "Toby telepop?" she asked.

Pradeep sighed, and then pulled a piece of paper and a pencil out of one of his pockets and drew an exact diagram of how it would work.

"If we can catch Fang at the exact moment she is trying to zombify the TV audience *and* get Frankie directly in front of the talent-transmission device when the scanner is turned on, then the zombification power should go directly to him," Pradeep said.

"OK." Geeky Girl paused. "I get it now. Of course I can help you configure the settings on the scanner and make some kind of talent-transmission satellite dish. How hard can it be? Hey, I bet we could raid the Lost Property room to get some materials for the device."

Pradeep was in full brainstorming mode. "We need a couple of bits from the inside of some cell phones, some aluminium foil, a radio and an umbrella."

"But if you blast the whole room with stolen pet powers, how can you make sure that people don't end up getting the talents instead of the pets?" I asked.

"I can calibrate the frequency to resonate at a level that only pets can absorb," said Pradeep.

I looked at him.

"The talent-transmission device will only affect pets, not people." Pradeep sighed.

Geeky Girl smiled and punched Pradeep on the arm again. "We make a good team, Brainiac."

"Ouch!" Pradeep said.

I think the social interaction part of his brain hadn't powered up again yet—or it could just have been Pradeep's way of saying out loud what his look was saying, which was: "I'm really glad that you approve of my plan and can support its implementation with your technological skills."

To be honest, "Ouch" was better.

"Right," I said. "I totally believe that you can get this scanner and talent-transmission satellite thing to work, but how are we going to get back into the school grounds, get the scanner onto the stage *and* get all the other pets back here for the show?"

"That's up to you, Tom," Pradeep said. "I thought up the hard stuff."

I shrugged my shoulders. "OK, let's get into action mode."

Pradeep and I immediately took off our ties (our moms had made us wear ties to the audition so we looked presentable) and tied them around our heads, Rambo-style, so we were ready for action. Sami and Geeky Girl looked at us like we were nuts.

"It helps get me into character," Pradeep said.

"First, Boris, you need to fly around to all the pet owners from today and drop them a note to say that they need to bring their pets back for the recording tonight."

"Does he need one of those cute little mailbags and a postman's cap?" Geeky Girl asked.

"I don't think he does . . . but if he would feel more comfortable with . . ." I stopped myself. "You were being sarcastic."

Geeky Girl smiled and said, "I'm sure Boris *could* deliver notes, but if you happened to have everyone's e-mail addresses I could just inbox them all, telling them to come."

"Or we could do that," I said.

"We need to get the clipboard from that lady who threw us out. I think she was the casting director. Her clipboard will definitely have everyone's information," Pradeep said.

"Boris, can you get the piece of paper with the details of everyone who auditioned today from that clipboard?" I asked.

Boris flapped his wings in agreement.

"Sami, I need you to look upset and to tell the security guards that you are lost and need to call home. They'll open the gates long enough for us

to sneak in and get inside the school building," I added.

Sami nodded. "I take Toby too," she said, hugging the tortoise.

I turned to Pradeep. "Once we're inside, you and Geeky Girl can sneak into the hall, make your talent-transmission device and get the cables all wired up."

"Check," said Pradeep.

"Frankie and I will head up to the lab room. We'll figure out a way to get one of the scanners down to you in time."

Boris flapped into the air toward the audition trailer.

A minute later we heard a shriek of "That bird attacked my clipboard!" and we saw Boris fly out of a window holding a piece of paper. One of the security guards headed back into the trailer leaving only one guard on the gate.

Boris landed on Geeky Girl's shoulder. "Thanks, Boris." She stroked his head as she

plucked the sheet of paper from his beak.

Sami was up next. The security guard was standing with his back to her. Geeky Girl, Pradeep and I hid in a bush just out of sight.

Sami tugged on the jacket of the guard through the fence. "Mr. Guard?" she whimpered.

He turned around and looked at her. She snuffled and her bottom lip quivered as she spoke. Man, that kid was good!

"I lost," she said. "Me and Toby all alone . . ." She held out her tortoise and I swear that tortoise looked just as sad and pathetic as Sami. I had no idea that tortoises could act!

The guard opened the gate right away. "Of course I can help you," he said. "You poor little thing. Did your friends leave you all by yourself?

We'll just get to a phone and call your mommy."
As he led Sami gently by the hand toward the
trailers, we all snuck through the gate before it
shut.

"Phew," I said. "Stage One complete. We are
in the zone."

"Check," said Pradeep again.

"Are you guys gonna do this mission stuff the
whole time, 'cause I can tell ya right now it's
gonna bug me," Geeky Girl said. "Let's just get
on with the plan."

CHAPTER 9
THE PLAN IS AFOOT

Pradeep and Geeky Girl headed for the back
door of the school hall where they were going to
start work on the transmission device and e-mail
everyone. Now it was down to Frankie and me
to get the scanner down two flights of stairs and
across the parking lot.

This was starting to feel like the bit of the plan
that might not work.

The door to the school building was still open
when we arrived. I carried Frankie up the stairs
in his bucket and carefully checked the room to
make sure no one was there.

Mark's bag was on one of the lab tables.

I looked inside. "Maybe there's a 'How To' manual for the scanners, or a diagram of his evil plan?" I said to Frankie.

Frankie rolled his eyes and then pointed a fin at the bag. But there wasn't a "How To" book in sight. Just some kitten toys, a ball of string, some chewing gum, an issue of *Evil Scientist* and Mark's usual anti-hypno stuff, contact lenses, goggles and a strip of photo booth pics of Mark and Fang.

"What?" I asked Frankie. "I don't get it . . ."

Frankie flipped into the bag and grabbed something with his teeth. "Oh! I see!" I said, suddenly understanding his plan.

A few minutes later I walked

up to the nearest of the two scanners. It was *big*
and it was *heavy*. There was no way I could lift
it, even with Frankie's help. It would take two
grown-ups, at least, to carry it. Two big grown-
ups like . . . the security guards!

"Frankie, we have to get the security guards
to carry the scanner to the school hall for us," I
said. "We'll need one of their walkie-talkies and
a bit of help from Geeky Girl."

Before we left, I grabbed a few more things
from Mark's bag. Then I turned over Mark's
"Scanning Room Closed" sign and wrote:

PRop For
My Pet's Got TaLeNt
movE to stAge

I hung it on one of the scanners and headed
down the stairs.

*

Frankie and I set up "Operation Walkie-Talkie" just inside the building entrance.

The first thing I did was to stick one end of the ball of string to the top of the door frame with chewing gum. I tied the other end to Frankie's tail and left Frankie's bucket right next to the door.

"Are you ready, Frankie?" I asked him. He splashed me and winked.

Next I hid in the shadows behind some boxes, waiting for the security guards to patrol the area. As soon as I heard them approaching, I rolled one of Fang's toy balls with a bell inside across the floor to attract their attention.

"What was that?" one of the guards said. They both hurried into the hallway.

The moment the second guard walked through the doorway, Frankie leaped out of his bucket and managed to flip himself onto the top of the door frame.

"Did you just hear something?" asked

the second guard. "It sounded like a fish . . . flipping?" He looked suspiciously at Frankie's bucket, but it was empty.

At that moment, I rolled the second bell ball. While the first guard followed the sound toward the stairs, Frankie swung down past the back of the second guard, grabbed the walkie-talkie from his belt with his teeth and swung up again to land back on top of the door frame.

Operation Walkie-Talkie had worked like clockwork (if by that you mean like a giant grandfather clock with a goldfish for a pendulum).

"There's nothing here," said the first guard, sounding slightly disappointed. "Let's go and have a cup of tea." They both hurried out and started walking back toward the trailers.

"Well done, Frankie," I whispered as I held up the bucket for him to jump back into.

I made sure the coast was clear, then tiptoed toward the back door of the school hall to try and find the others. Inside, I found Pradeep plugging wires and cables into a satellite dish made of stuff they had scavenged from the Lost Property room, while Geeky Girl was tapping away on a computer keyboard.

"Nearly got it," Pradeep said, jamming a black cable into place.

"That looks, er . . . interesting," I said. I turned to Geeky Girl and explained what I needed her to do.

"Undercover work is my middle name," she said. "Actually, it's Imelda, but if you tell anyone that I'll have to kill you." She took the walkie-talkie and barked into it. "Security! Casting to Security! Where are you people?"

Static filled the airwaves then a panicked voice came through. "Sorry, we were doing our rounds for the night and—"

"I don't care," Geeky Girl snapped. "Go to the science building and get that prop scanner down here for the show, pronto!"

"Pronto?" I mouthed to Geeky Girl.

"We'll get it right away. Over." They signed off.

"Over and out." Geeky Girl said, then tossed the walkie-talkie back to me. "Like taking candy from a baby."

We hid behind the stage curtains until the guards arrived carrying the scanner.

"She said to put it here," one security guard said.

"I definitely don't want her yelling at me again," said the other. "I left that little girl sitting at the front gate with the receptionist. She couldn't remember her phone number, so we're waiting to see if her friends come back. I'd better go and check on her."

I shot Pradeep a look that said, *"Sami!* I'll go

and get her while you and Geeky Girl get the scanner hooked up and ready to go."

"OK!" his look replied. "I hope this works."

I picked up the bucket with Frankie in it and backed away from the curtains as the guards headed off the stage and out of the hall. Suddenly I bumped into something large and solid.

I turned around and was face to face—well, more like face to shoulder—with Mark!

"Going somewhere?" he asked. "You don't want to miss Fang's TV debut, do you?"

Pradeep and Geeky Girl must have heard Mark's voice, as they'd vanished so I couldn't see them at all. I immediately slapped my hand over the top of Frankie's bucket so he couldn't jump out. I couldn't risk him being caught now. Then the plan would stand no chance of working.

Mark did an evil laugh, which was frightening enough, but as he stepped into the light I realized his face had turned zombie goldfish orange!

"Mark, have you been in the scanner?" I

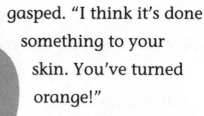

gasped. "I think it's done something to your skin. You've turned orange!"

Mark loomed over me like the scary, orange, Evil Scientist big brother he was. "It's the make-up," he growled. "For the TV." He leaned closer. "You tell anyone and you are soooo pummeled."

"No one," I said, shaking my head.

Then Fang poked her head out from Mark's pocket. She was wearing a diamond-studded cat collar and looked like she had been professionally cat-fluffed.

"Um, Mark . . ." I started to say, when from behind him stepped Sami, still carrying Toby the tortoise.

She was staring at my left shoe with one eye

and at the stage door with the other. "Pretty little kitty," she chanted over and over.

My look screamed, "Nooooooooooooooooooooo!"

But no one was there to read my face.

CHAPTER 10
PRETTY LITTLE (EVIL) KITTY

"Don't you like what Fang has done to Sami?"
asked Mark. "I saw the receptionist walking her
up to the front gate desk when I was coming
back with Fang from make-up. I knew you had
to be up to something, and I wasn't going to
have any morons, big or little, ruin things this
time."

Fang jumped up onto Mark's shoulder and
purred.

"Besides, we needed to test Fang's new
hypnotic powers to make sure they really
worked. The receptionist at the gate let Sami
come with us right away when cute little Fang

stared into her eyes. She'll tell the security guards that the little girl's mom came and picked her up, but she will stare at his left shoe and the wall when she says it."

Mark stuck his hand in front of the tortoise and it snapped at him. Toby was clearly not zombified.

"We tried to get the tortoise too," he muttered, "but who knew that tortoise shells are hypno-proof? Never mind, it can't do anything interesting anyway." Mark peered at Toby.

"Eating lettuce? What kind of talent is that? They even cut it from Fang's final act."

Toby actually looked a little hurt by that bit.

I waved my hand in front of Sami's face. "Sami? Can you hear me?" but she just kept chanting.

I glared up at my evil big brother.

"You won't get away with this!"

"Really?" Mark said. "I don't think your little fishy friend can stop me, can he?"

Even though I'd been doing my best to keep Frankie in the bucket, he managed to burst out from under my fingers and throw himself at Mark. But before he could reach him, Fang leaped forward and the two pets tumbled to the floor, Frankie tail-slapping at the kitten while she swiped her claws at him.

"Ya know, I could watch this for hours but we've got a show to do." Mark scooped up Fang by the scruff of her neck and gently dropped her into his white lab-coat pocket. Frankie jumped back in his bucket. He tried to glare at Mark, but sighed when he remembered he'd lost his zombie powers and slumped down to the bottom of the water.

"The fish is pretty useless now . . ." Mark looked at me and smiled. "But just in case you aren't, I should take care of you."

Fang leaped back up onto Mark's shoulder and glared at me. Her eyes glowed a deep zombie green. I closed my eyes tight, but Mark stomped hard on my sneaker and when I opened my eyes again, Fang was right in front of my face staring hard.

"Pretty little kitty," I chanted. One of my eyes looked at Mark's left shoe and the other stared at the stage curtains.

"Result." Mark smirked and Fang purred.

CHAPTER 11
THE SHOW MUST SCAN ON

Just then, the casting-director lady came running up to Mark. "What was that shouting?" She looked at me. "How did he get in here? Is he causing any problems?"

"No, that's just my little moron . . . I mean, my little *brother*." Mark smiled. "He wanted to stay and watch the show. He won't be any trouble now. And this is my friend's little sister. She's a big fan."

"Good," the casting director said. "The audience are all seated and Solomon Caldwell has just arrived. We need to get you and that talented kitten in the green room with the other contestants, ready for the start of the show. We are live on air in five minutes and you're up first!" Then she leaned into Mark and whispered, "Your kitten is a shoo-in to win this. None of the other pets that made the show are even close to her level of talent."

Fang meowed a proud (and evil) meow.

Sami and I were still quietly chanting, "Pretty little kitty."

"Ahh, that's sweet," the casting director said. "They really are big fans of the kitten."

She rushed Mark away with Fang still purring on his shoulder, a slight green glint in her eyes. Sami toddled after them.

Suddenly Pradeep and Geeky Girl swung down from the curtain rails. So that's where they had hidden when Mark came in!

Boris flew down and sat on the edge of Frankie's bucket.

"Tom! Tom! Speak to me!" cried Pradeep, shaking me by the shoulders. He shook me so

hard I thought I
would keel over.

"He's a kitten
zombie slave
now," Geeky
Girl said sadly.
"There's nothing
we can do."

"Noooooo!"
cried Pradeep. "He
was my best friend!"

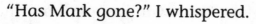

"Has Mark gone?" I whispered.

"What?" said Pradeep.

"Has Mark gone?" I whispered again.

"Yes," Geeky Girl said, looking around.

"Phew, it worked!" I smiled.

Pradeep's look said, "What worked?" But it
said it in a very loud and kinda irritated way.

"Mark's hypno-proof contact lenses. I found
them in Mark's bag. I thought I should put them
in, just in case I got a little too close to Fang."

Frankie splashed me from his bucket.

"Well, it was more Frankie's idea," I admitted.

"Is Sami wearing them too?" Pradeep asked.

"No, he got her for real," I said. "Sorry."

We could see the casting director seating Sami in the audience between the kid with the roller-skating beagle and Rabbit Girl. She was holding Toby and a bottle of water on her lap. "At least she's safe for now," Pradeep said.

"Now that Mark thinks I'm a zombie slave, he won't be worried if I get close to Fang," I added. "Is the scanner all wired up and ready to go?"

"Yep," Pradeep said. He picked up Frankie's bucket and tied one of the curtain ropes to the handle. "Geeky Girl and I will keep hiding above the stage. Frankie can hide with us too. He'll give Mark and Fang a wet surprise when we need him too, won't you, Frankie?"

Frankie tail-fived Pradeep.

"Boris, are you good on your part of the plan?" Geeky Girl asked. Boris cawed quietly and then flitted back up into the curtains while Pradeep and Geeky Girl climbed up the ladder at the side of the stage.

I went and stood by the green-room door. Mark and Fang would be coming out any second, so I made sure to keep mumbling "Pretty little kitty."

Meanwhile Solomon Caldwell, the famous talent show host, appeared just by my side. He smoothed his mustache, tucked his T-shirt carefully into his trousers, flicked a touch of dust from his jacket lapel and strode out onto the stage.

"Hello"—he paused—". . . wherever we are!" and the audience laughed and clapped.

"Now the show is about to start, and *boy*, do we have an impressive example of pet talent from your hometown tonight! You won't believe your eyes!"

Mark and Fang walked out of the green room behind me, and Solomon glanced over. A look of "I've seen you somewhere before but I just can't place you" came across his face. Then he turned back to the crowd.

"So, my lovely audience, in the next moment or so this little green light will come on and that means that we are broadcasting live." He pointed to a light on the camera. "Just keep your reactions natural when we're on air and please, no begging for autographs or photos." The audience laughed again. "I didn't mean *my* autograph, I meant the paw prints of all the talented pets we have on! Say it with me . . ."

As the theme music started and the green light

came on, the audience said together, "MY PET'S GOT *TALENT!*"

Solomon Caldwell led them in their applause and then silenced them with his "on air" welcome speech.

I looked up and winked at Pradeep and Geeky Girl. Frankie flicked down a little drop of water from his bucket up out of sight above the stage. We were ready for action!

CHAPTER 12
FANG'S BIG NIGHT

"Our first act of the night is a multitalented little kitty from just around the corner," said Solomon once the applause had died down. "She's called Fang, although if I were naming her I would definitely call her 'Cutie Pie.'"

Fang winced and bared her teeth when Solomon said "Cutie Pie," and I could hear Mark whispering, "Never mind that, Fang. Please don't attack the host. Just think of the lifetime's supply of catnip and world domination!"

"Let's see what this talented little cat can do," Solomon went on, motioning to Mark to set Fang down on a pedestal that had been placed

in front of the backdrop (which was hiding the scanner and our talent-transmission device from Mark, Fang and the audience).

Next to the pedestal was a canvas on an easel and some paints, as well as a dish of bubble mixture. Solomon walked off to the side of the stage with Mark while Fang sat still, cleaning her paws.

"Awwwwww!" The audience sighed.

Mark waved at Fang and she leaped off the pedestal. Underneath were some roller skates. She jumped into them and started skating around the stage with ease.

The audience "Oohed" and "Aahed," and I swear I could see the lips of the boy with the beagle mumbling, "She's not as good as Charlie." He patted his floppy-eared, disappointed-looking dog.

Next Fang stepped out of the roller skates and pushed a top hat out from under the pedestal. She stuck her head inside and pulled out a very surprised-looking rabbit by the scruff of its neck.

Most of the audience went "Oooooohhhhhhh."
Except for Rabbit Girl, who I think was saying,
"*That's* where Roy went!"

Fang jumped back into the roller skates and
started meowing the tune to *Star Wars*. At the
same time she licked
up a little bit of bubble
mix and blew Mona
Lisa–shaped
bubbles in the
air. As if
this wasn't
enough,
she was also
using her tail
to paint a
few strokes on
the canvas each
time she skated past. It was emerging as a lovely
French Impressionist sunset.

The ferret in the audience scrambled onto its owner's head to get a better look. Then it tutted and pulled its beret down over his eyes.

The audience was captivated. They couldn't get enough. Solomon Caldwell leaned into Mark and I could hear him saying, "I've never seen an audience so mesmerized by an act before!"

Mark smiled and a tiny evil laugh escaped. He covered it up like he was clearing his throat.

"Mwhaa, haa, um, ahem, ahem!" He smiled at Solomon. "Yeah, *mesmerized*. You have no idea how mesmerized they'll *all* be by the end." He snapped his fingers.

Fang jumped out of the skates and onto the pedestal, her eyes starting to brighten with a green glow. She was going into full zombie stare mode!

Boris spotted the change right away and cawed to Geeky Girl to signal it was time. Then he flew out into the audience just as Pradeep and Geeky Girl pulled up the backdrop from

behind Fang, revealing the scanner.

Geeky Girl's e-mail to the owners of pets that had had their talents stolen had told them *exactly* what to do when they saw Boris fly in during the show.

Right on cue, they released their pets. In seconds the stage was filled with a swarm of jumping, running, hopping and scampering animals.

Solomon Caldwell rushed back onstage to try and calm everything down, but was met by Tugger the ferret, who ran up his trouser leg, climbed around inside his suit jacket and eventually appeared on the top of Solomon's head.

Mark shouted to Fang, "Just keep up the stare, Fang. Keep going!"

"Now!" I yelled, giving up my zombie act, and Pradeep tipped Frankie's bucket right on top of Fang.

As the water hit her she wailed, "MEEEEEEEEEEEEEW!" If there is one thing that

kittens hate even more than zombie goldfish, it's water. So water containing a zombie goldfish has to be the ultimate kitten nightmare!

Fang leaped off the pedestal and landed right inside the open scanner behind her, desperate to avoid the water.

I slammed shut the lid while Geeky Girl threw the switch to set the scanner going, and a buzzing, charging sound filled the stage.

Frankie was flipping around on the floor as Mark rushed up to try and break Fang free. I had to stop him! I grabbed the first thing that I could—the sunset canvas that Fang had painted—and bopped Mark over the head.

The canvas broke when it hit his head (which only slowed him down a little) but then I pulled the frame down over his shoulders so he couldn't lift up his arms to open the lid of the scanner.

"Nooooo!" Mark shouted as I hung onto the frame, keeping him trapped.

Pradeep and Geeky Girl were busy attempting to round up the rest of the pets, so it was up to me to get Frankie in front of the talent-transmission device thingy that Pradeep had rigged up so he would get his zombie powers back.

But I couldn't let go of the canvas frame or Mark would get away!

CHAPTER 13

A MENAGERIE OF MULTITALENTED PETS

The whole stage was in chaos. The easel had fallen over, the beagle was carrying Toby around in his mouth like an oversized chew toy, the two rabbits were fighting over the top hat, and the ferret on Solomon's head had pulled off the host's toupee and run off with it.

Solomon quickly grabbed the top hat from one of the rabbits and put it on to cover his bald head.

"Boris!" I yelled, as Mark jerked around, trying to escape from the frame. "You need to get Frankie in front of the scanner . . . now!"

"Caw!" Boris replied. He swooped down and

grabbed Frankie by the tail. Then he held him right in front of the talent-transmission device, just as the scanner had powered up to full.

"Way to go, Boris!" Geeky Girl whooped from the other side of the stage. "That's my bird!"

A buzz came out of the transmitter and all the animals onstage immediately stopped what they were doing as their fur or feathers stood on end with a static-electric charge.

"Noooooo!" yelled Mark.

Boris dropped Frankie and shook out his own feathers as if he had had a tiny electric shock.

Frankie flopped down on top of the scanner, twitched, and opened his eyes. They were his own powerful zombie green once more!

The sound quieted as the machine finished and turned itself off.

By now the casting director and security guards had all jumped up onstage and were trying to shoo the animals back to their seats. Solomon was attempting to wrestle his toupee back off the ferret, and the audience was laughing and clapping as if they had never seen anything so funny in all their lives.

I guess they thought this was all part of the show.

Sami jumped up from her seat. "Naughty little kitty!" she said as she ran up onto the stage. "Swishy fishy OK?"

She had her bottle of water with her. I finally

let go of the frame that was trapping Mark, grabbed Frankie's bucket and poured the water into it.

Frankie jumped in and swam around. He looked happier than I've ever seen him.

At the same time Mark pulled himself free of the frame. He opened the lid of the scanner and picked up Fang. "Are you OK?" he said to the tired-looking kitten. "Go on, zombify them all! Let them have it!"

Fang squinted and tried her best to do a zombie glare but nothing came.

While Mark was distracted, Pradeep and Geeky Girl looped some strong curtain rope around him, trapping his arms by his sides for the second time in less than five minutes.

"As you would say, Mark," Pradeep said, "Result!"

Frankie was just about to leap out of the bucket and go for Fang when I stopped him.

"Wait a second, Frankie. Does anything seem

different to you?" I looked around at the other animals on the stage. Pradeep, Sami and Geeky Girl looked around too.

Charlie the beagle was painting what looked like a dog bone floating through a sky full of clouds on the stage floor.

Tugger the ferret was doing magic tricks while sitting on Solomon Caldwell's shoulder, and had pulled Solomon's toupee out of the top hat.

The bunnies, Siegfried and Roy, were now each in one roller skate and doing a very complicated roller-dance routine, weaving in and out of the other pets.

All the pets seemed happy with their new talents.

Solomon Caldwell took his toupee from the

ferret, readjusted it and walked to the center of the stage. He looked like he was about to scream at the casting director, so she quickly pointed at the green light on the camera. "We are still *live* on TV!" she mouthed.

Instead Solomon smiled his Hollywood smile and said, "Well, that was a big surprise! We went from one talented little cat to a whole room full of talented pets. That just goes to show that you can't keep a talented pet off the stage, can you?"

The audience clapped and cheered. I heard people saying, "This is the best *My Pet's Got Talent* ever!," "I'm going to watch every week if the show is this good!" and "That was the funniest thing I've seen on TV in ages!"

The casting director was listening to something on her headset. Then she held up a sign saying "Go to Commercial Break."

The green light went off and the casting director rushed onto the stage.

"The viewing figures are through the roof!"

she squealed. "There are already millions of hits on our website where we've posted a clip from the show. And more people tuned in in the last three minutes than have watched *all season* put together. We've gone viral!"

Solomon Caldwell grinned. Then he whispered. "But what about my hair?"

"Everyone thinks it was staged for the show. They love it!" the casting director said.

Geeky Girl and Pradeep came over to stand with me and Sami and Frankie. Solomon looked over at us with that same look of "I've seen you before—but where?"

Then he looked at Frankie. "Of course, *Robin Hood*!" he said, coming over and shaking our hands and patting Frankie on the head. "You were in that strange but brilliant school production of *Robin Hood* I saw here with the flying goldfish. Thanks for making this such an exciting show."

Fang had managed to chew Mark free of the

curtain rope and they stumbled over to Solomon.

"What about Fang winning the show?" Mark said. "She was the most talented pet, right? So she must still win?"

"Let's see what she can do when we go back on air . . . now that she has a lot more competition up here," Solomon said, looking around at the talented pets that surrounded him.

"Come and take a seat in the audience," the casting director said, ushering the rest of us to seats. "We need to get started again."

The green light came back on just as the casting director ducked out of shot.

"Welcome back to the second half of tonight's show. As you all know, we've met some super-talented pets already this evening, so let's recap what they can all do before we meet the rest of tonight's contestants and choose a winner to go to the *grand final*!"

He read from a card the casting director had passed him.

"This is Charlie, the painting beagle." The crowd cheered.

"This is Tugger, the ferret magician." The crowd clapped.

"These clever little bunnies are Siegfried and Roy, and just look at them skate!" he went on as the crowd oohed.

"And of course we have lovely little Cutie Pie . . ." Fang sharpened her claws. "I mean Fang, who . . ."

The camera panned over to Fang, who was sitting on the pedestal munching on some lettuce. "No way, *that's* the talent you're left with?" I heard Mark cry. Unable to take the humiliation, he ran out onstage and picked up Fang. "Come on, girl! Do something *really evil* for your talent, at least?"

As if on cue, Fang threw up the lettuce all over Mark.

"She . . ." Solomon continued, "has a very interesting talent *indeed*."

"It smells *really evil*," I said to Pradeep.

We watched the rest of the show and cheered for the talented pets from the audience. Boris sat on Geeky Girl's shoulder and Toby sat on Sami's lap as we waited for the final vote.

"And the winner is . . ." Solomon spoke as the drum rolled. "Well, this hasn't happened before! It's a three-way tie between Charlie, Tugger, and Siegfried and Roy!"

The audience went wild as Mark and Fang slowly crept off the stage. Mark glared at us and Fang hissed at Frankie.

Frankie flipped out of his bucket for a moment and let his eyes glow slightly green, which made

Fang's eyes go red with rage. Then he flopped back down and floated in a chilled-out pose on his back.

"I think Frankie is done with talent shows," I said to Pradeep.

"Me too," said Pradeep. "Come on, Sami, time to go home."

As we got up to go, Geeky Girl asked, "What about Mark and Fang? Are we going to just let them get away?"

"I heard the casting director say that the Internet clip of Fang throwing up on Mark has over two million views already," Pradeep answered.

Geeky Girl was already on her smartphone.

"Yup, it's called *Creepy Orange Kid versus Kitten Barf-fest*." She paused. "Nice title."

"Mark has to go to school tomorrow knowing that every kid in the country has watched that video again and again and again." I added. "That's gotta be punishment enough."

As we said good-bye to Geeky Girl outside, I couldn't help but notice that Boris wasn't hovering over her shoulder anymore. One moment he was there, but the next he was sitting on Frankie's bucket wing-fiving Frankie, then he was on Sami's shoulder saying good-bye to Toby, then almost instantly he was back on Geeky Girl's shoulder again.

"Did you just see what I saw?" Pradeep said to me.

I looked over at Toby, who was gently levitating over Sami's lap.

Geeky Girl stroked Boris's head. "There's something different about you, dude," she said.

"But you look happier than I've seen ya in ages, so it can't be bad."

"They all look happy," I said, looking at all the chilled-out pets around us.

"See you guys around sometime," Geeky Girl said. "Look after my favorite fish!" She leaned over Frankie's bucket. "And Frankie, you look after them, OK?"

Frankie splashed at her playfully and then Geeky Girl turned to Pradeep. "Well done, Brainiac. This would never have worked if you hadn't had the scanner reversal idea. We make a good team." She smiled at Pradeep and he went bright red. For a split second I actually thought that Geeky Girl was gonna give Pradeep a kiss on the cheek, but then she pulled back her fist and punched him on the arm again.

"Later, dudes," she said as she and Boris strolled away.

"Ouch!" said Pradeep as he watched her go.

Sami looked up at us and yawned. "Toby

tired," she said.

"I know," Pradeep said to her, and smiled. "Let's go home."

"Do you think Toby will miss the super-speed of being a teleporting tortoise?" I whispered to Pradeep as we walked away.

"I think after the scooter ride on the way here, the zip-line, and being thrown across a room, Toby will be happy to live his life in the slow lane for a while," Pradeep replied.

"At least for now," I said.

Thank you for reading this FEIWEL AND FRIENDS book.
The Friends who made

MY BIG FAT ZOMBIE GOLDFISH
LIVE AND LET SWIM

possible are:

JEAN FEIWEL, Publisher

LIZ SZABLA, Editor in Chief

RICH DEAS, Senior Creative Director

HOLLY WEST, Editor

ALEXEI ESIKOFF, Senior Managing Editor

KIM WAYMER, Production Manager

ANNA ROBERTO, Editor

CHRISTINE BARCELLONA, Associate Editor

EMILY SETTLE, Administrative Assistant

ANNA POON, Editorial Assistant

FOLLOW US ON FACEBOOK OR
VISIT US ONLINE AT MACKIDS.COM.

OUR BOOKS ARE FRIENDS FOR LIFE